# LIFE STUDY #2

*A Journey in Uncertain Times*

Helen Nicholl

First published 2024 by Owl's House Press



ISBN: 978-1-3999-7468-4

Cover image from an original painting by Kenneth Nicholl
Cover design: Helen Nicholl and Averill Buchanan

*'They change their sky, not their soul, who run across the sea...'*
Horace

# CATALOGUE NOTE

No 8. Life Study #2. This is an early work by Yassine Ayari. At its heart is the image of a young girl lying naked on a richly patterned rug, or kilim. Five floating figures surround her, one of them a painter at his easel. This central composition is itself contained within the borders of a map, the boundaries of whose countries, or regions, are marked in gold. On closer inspection, these demarcations turn out to be lines of poetry that run like veins of light across the darkness.

Some see in the map the outlines of Africa, others Europe, but the title provides no further clues to the meaning of the work. Of the floating figures, one (the painter) is thought to be Ayari himself and another the Irish poet Liam McMahon, whose words illuminate the canvas. Over the years, various theories and interpretations have been put forward as to the identity of the nude and the remaining figures, but as Ayari has always declined to speak about his work, this remains a matter for speculation.

# 1

*'Interesting, that,' says one of the two people in the gallery, turning from the catalogue to his companion. 'Bit of a change from today's self-publicists, but perhaps he felt great art should speak for itself?'*

*'Either that or he thought a bit of mystery would make him more sought after. Can't say I know much about him – Tunisian wasn't he? Or possibly Algerian? Although I seem to remember he studied in London ...'*

London. The first decade of the new century. Outside Somerset House, on the terrace above the Embankment, a couple are drinking coffee. The only other person sitting there is a boy called Yassine, who's waiting for the girl he hopes to take on a tour of the Courtauld Gallery. He's sketching the couple unobtrusively while he waits, partly because he's an art student and needs something to do, but mostly because he thinks it will impress the girl – if she turns up, which is starting to look unlikely.

Occasional snatches of conversation drift across over the distant rumble of traffic and the cries of the gulls overhead. From what he can make out, these two seem to be old friends, rather than husband and wife. The man looks like any middle-aged English gentleman: fair complexion, good tweed jacket, plain gold wedding ring. The woman is more casually dressed; she has darker, weathered skin and her thick, unruly hair is finely striped with grey. On the face of it an unremarkable older couple. But look again: the woman has an unusual face – not quite beautiful, but arresting, full of movement, as are the crooked hands whose rings catch the light as she gestures. The man appears to be listening with amusement ...

It has always surprised Anton that – in spite of everything – Olivia never seems to lose her zest for life. She's led such an unexpected, precarious existence (calamitous even) yet he can't think of anyone who relishes their own dramas more. Now, as she throws up her palms in mock despair at the story she's been telling, he has a sudden memory of one of those hands lying still for once, curled on his chest. Where had they been? Amsterdam? Istanbul? Somewhere with a river, at any rate: perhaps it's the sound of the gulls and the distant hooting of a ship that have reminded him.

'Well,' he says, 'it doesn't sound as though anything's changed.'

'Oh no, there *have* been changes, a lot of them for the better – why don't you come over and see for yourself? Mind you, it's still the only place in the UK that a woman can't get an abortion – there was someone prosecuted just the other day for buying pills online, for Christ's sake! Still, I always liked the place, God knows why ... not for the politics or the weather, that's for sure! Anyway,' she shrugs, 'it's home now, for better or worse – my final destination ...'

'What, no more travelling? What will you do? Take up gardening? Write your memoirs?' He raises an eyebrow. 'Why not? The rest of the world seems to be baring its collective soul these days – so why not you – at least your story would be genuinely entertaining!'

She shakes her head. 'Not a chance, Anton: too many of the supporting characters are still alive – I can't afford to get sued!'

(One of the chief supporting characters – a man called Jonathan Altman – has died, as it happens, just a moment or two earlier on the other side of the world, but as they don't yet know this, both Anton and Olivia laugh.)

Yassine, who already has a complicated history of his own, at this point checks his watch and resigns himself to the fact that the girl isn't coming. But as he closes his sketch pad, he hears the man say, 'When do you leave?'

'Tonight. In fact, I need to get going right now.' She drains her cup. 'I'll be away until the end of the month, but I meant it, why don't you come over when I get back? Bring Marie-Claude.'

Yassine wonders briefly where she's going, what her story is; she has the air of a woman used to attention. Perhaps she was once someone of importance. But she's old now, so who knows – or cares? And getting to his feet, he turns his back on them and heads off towards the river, and into the next chapter of his own unfolding story.

*

Olivia's story began several decades ago, in a very different time and place: 6,000 miles away, to be precise, in South Africa.

There's a picture in the family album of the baby in her mother's arms, wrapped in trailing lace to be christened with her good, traditional names: Olivia Grace. Even at a few months old, she bears a strong resemblance to her Aunt Ianthe, the family beauty, which should have been a warning, but her parents, who have survived the war – and their own considerable tragedies – smile down on her, untroubled. Only little fair-haired Cynthia looks sombre. She has her head slightly cocked, as though listening to something – possibly alarm bells ringing faintly in the future.

The album came to light in the great clear-out of Cynthia's house, and was put aside by Harriet, Cynthia's eldest daughter. 'We thought you might like to have this one,' Harriet told her aunt. 'It's full of photos of you and Mummy when you were little.'

Olivia, newly arrived from London, still sleep-deprived and disorientated from the long flight to Cape Town, can't help feeling that Cynthia's life is being tidied away with indecent haste (she's not even dead yet) but she looks through the album. Among the studio portraits, and faded snapshots of family gatherings and celebrations, are photographs of long-gone domestic workers, of nameless babies, forgotten cats. And here is one of Cynthia and Olivia in the checked dresses and Panama hats of St Anne's, on their first day at their new school. Olivia, aged eight or nine, is scowling; Cynthia, three years older, has the serene and exalted expression of one about to be translated into heaven, because St Anne's represents everything that she and her mother both yearn for. Olivia, on the other hand, knows she will hate it, and duly does.

If Mrs Martin were still alive (God forbid) she might remember Anton's mother – solid, pleasant, entirely unremarkable Mrs de Waal – stopping in the street to ask if it was true: were the Martins really going to move to Cape Town? It was plain that Mrs de Waal couldn't understand why anyone in their right minds would want to leave their little seaside town – a safe twenty miles distant from all the dangers and expense of the city – but she was too polite to say so.

Olivia's mother, on the other hand, had no shred of doubt. She'd waged a long, hard battle to get her husband to agree to the move, but the moment when her plans finally came to fruition was one that she would never forget ...

She is pinning a paper dress pattern to a length of cloth spread out on the table. Beside the door leading into the kitchen, Lizzie (delinquent daughter of their maid, Florence) is ironing sheets, while through the open dining-room window children's voices can be heard, against the distant sound of the neighbour's radio.

'There may be enough of this left over for you, Lizzie,' Mrs Martin says kindly. 'It might even be enough for a blouse.' She looks doubtfully at Lizzie, who is disconcertingly well-developed, but she wants to say something that will cheer the girl up.

'Yes Madam.' Lizzie is supposed to call her 'Mrs Martin' not 'Madam' (a term Mrs Martin dislikes) but she never does.

Mrs Martin sighs. She's made several attempts to engage Lizzie in conversation but has had no success. This is all the more distressing because she sees herself as someone who has suffered a great deal and is therefore especially sympathetic to others. Not that Lizzie appears to be suffering, but her mother is.

'You seem to be ironing those quite nicely.' (This isn't true, but Mrs Martin is not a woman who gives up easily.) 'I'm sure your mother will miss your help when you go home tomorrow, but she'll be happy to know you're back at school. She worries about you, Lizzie, but it's a comfort to her to know you're living with your grandmother. It's just such a pity that we have these terrible laws in our country and that you can't stay here with your mother. But we must all pray that one day things will change, and that all our children will go to school together.'

Lizzie looks mutinous but says nothing. She has no intention of going back to school tomorrow, or ever. She also thinks Mrs Martin is a crazy woman, and that her dress fabric is horrible, but she hopes she'll get a couple of coins if she keeps quiet and finishes the sheets.

'Lizzie, would you leave those for a minute please, and go and check on the children.' Mrs Martin has noticed suddenly that the children's voices have faded while the noise from next door's radio has increased. She vaguely recognises the voice of Doris Day – not that she has any interest in popular music. The Martins prefer classical. 'Make sure Olivia isn't playing near the pond.'

Lizzie puts down the iron, wipes her nose with the back of her hand, and pads out of the kitchen, tight pink skirt straining across her buttocks. Mrs Martin sincerely believes what she's just said about hoping that all South Africa's multi-coloured children will one day go to school together, but she suffers a momentary qualm at the thought of Lizzie in the uniform of St Anne's. This is the private school she hopes both Cynthia and Olivia will eventually attend, although Mr Martin has so far proved resistant. His wife, however, is confident that she will eventually persuade him. She has been sustained since childhood by her faith in God's mysterious ways (apparent to her, if not to her husband) which are always, in the end, for the best. She puts in another pin and murmurs, 'All shall be well, and all manner of things shall be well' – she is fond of quoting Julien of Norwich to herself, and to those of her friends who share her spiritual sensitivities.

And it is at precisely this moment, as Olivia remembers her mother so often saying, that a voice in her head tells her very clearly to phone St Anne's NOW. Which she does, to be told by the Headmistress's secretary that a most unexpected vacancy has arisen.

'It's quite extraordinary that you should have phoned at this particular moment,' says the woman. 'I was just about to look at the waiting list, but as you are on the line, I think we might offer the place to you first. Yes, it is for next year, and Cynthia would be eligible to board. How old is she? Oh, many of our girls start even earlier: they soon settle down, you know, and being a boarder does give them a far greater sense of belonging. We do have daygirls of course, but one always feels they are never *quite* so much a part of things.'

The secretary allows a little pause, during which Mrs Martin sees Cynthia's chances of becoming Form Captain, a Prefect, Head Girl – and herself the gracious, smiling observer of these achievements – all slip away, just because she didn't board. So she replies that of course she will have to consult her husband, but she thinks they can take it as agreed that Cynthia will start at St Anne's next year. And her younger sister? Yes, it appears that Olivia will be accepted too.

*

In the end Mr Martin had baulked at the expense of boarding and both girls were enrolled as day scholars, but his wife consoled herself with the thought that after all, the camaraderie of the dormitory was not as important for daughters as the watchful eye of their mother. (Not that this would do any good in the case of Olivia, but Mrs Martin, thanks to the infinite mercy of her Creator, was unable to look into the future and therefore remained in happy ignorance of what was to come.)

# 2

If Yassine were going to tell his story (he won't, although in time many books will be written about him) he'd say that dwelling on the past is a waste of time. For him, the future is all that matters. His sponsor, a wealthy family friend, gets a brief letter once a term, informing her of his progress. She keeps these letters, which are illustrated with small sketches of London life, in a cedar-wood box (a wise move: they'll fetch a considerable sum of money one day) and looks forward to the day when the beautiful boy will return – and, she very much hopes, resume the weekly visits that in his teenage years gave her such illicit pleasure. But in this she will be disappointed, because Yassine hasn't the slightest intention of returning: luck and talent have brought him to London; hard work will take him further.

A few days after his meeting with Olivia, Anton, stopping for a coffee on his way to work, noticed that the boy who took his order gave him a smile of what looked like recognition.

'You're not one of my students, are you? I have trouble remembering faces these days.'

The young man smiles. 'No. I am art student.'

'Ah. I teach History. Anton de Waal.'

'Yassine,' says the student, and disappears back inside. But when he brings the coffee, he also hands Anton a page, torn from a sketch book.

'I have seen you at the Courtauld – you and the lady. Here.'

The sketch is remarkable: Olivia, caught in strong, sure lines, intensely alive, gesturing.

'You can keep,' says the boy.

Anton's hand moves towards his wallet, 'Please, let me buy it!' but the boy waves him away.

'That's extraordinarily generous,' says Anton. 'Here, let me give you my card. You never know—'

The young man scrutinises the card. 'Thank you,' he says. Then, producing a pen, he takes the sketch back from Anton, and signs it. This too, will fetch a surprising sum of money, if Anton ever decides to sell it.

A week or two later, he looks up from his desk to see Patrick Luke lounging elegantly in the doorway. Patrick, as well as being Marie-Claude's cousin, is an old friend – and a famous one to boot – and as such is confident of his welcome, however unexpected his arrival.

Anton leans back in his chair, regarding him quizzically. 'I must have forgotten to lock the door.'

Patrick grins. 'No. Marie-Claude was just ahead of me. She's making us some coffee. Well, old friend, how are you?' And he draws up a chair, swings his booted feet up onto the desk, and settles in for a chat.

Anton gives an inward sigh – work is over for the day – but Patrick hasn't passed through London for a while, and despite himself Anton is always flattered at being sought out. There's a lot to catch up on too: Patrick's latest film, Anton's work and family, mutual friends.

'By the way, I saw Olivia Martin a couple of weeks ago,' Anton says, 'and oddly enough, there was an art student nearby—' He proceeds to tell Patrick about the boy, and the sketch, which he brings out from a drawer in his desk.

'Well, well,' says Patrick, 'Olivia! I haven't seen her for a while.' He peers at the signature. 'Yassine Ayari – or something like that. This boy appears to have unusual talent – a different class entirely from Olivia's stuff! Although I do have to admit that I've always liked her travel books, particularly the one she did on Rome. If only she hadn't seen fit to create Pontificat!' (Over the years, Olivia has produced several quirky, illustrated travel books, but success had come with the unlikely fame of a feline character called Paddycat.)

'Olivia didn't create Paddycat,' says Anton, 'as you very well know. She merely illustrates his adventures.'

Paddycat, a rotund philosopher who travels the world, is beloved by generations of toddlers and loathed by Patrick – himself reputed to be named after an Anglo-Irish grandfather with a castle in Meath. Despite Patrick's assertions that the stories are ill-disguised sermons, in reality they're as unremittingly cheerful and simple in nature as their aged author, a one-time nun. And they've always been redeemed, in Anton's eyes at least, by the anarchic humour of Olivia's drawings.

'Well, you'll be glad to know both Paddycat and his creator have had their day,' he says now. 'And Olivia seems to have had enough too – she's thinking of retirement in a cottage with a dog.'

'I find that somewhat hard to picture!' Patrick raises an eyebrow. 'I saw that Jonathan Altman has died, by the way. Did she say anything about him?'

'Strangely enough, he died the same day this sketch was done.' He gestures at the drawing. 'The news didn't get out until later, but she was flying out to Cape Town that night, so no doubt she's found out by now.'

'What a very long time ago it all was!' says Patrick. 'Mind you, I still have a vivid memory of that day we first met. Olivia was memorable even then – although I was far more interested in you, of course!'

Anton remembers the occasion all too well. A wild, bright, winter's day, when he'd been invited to tea with Gerald and Angus Bailey at their grandmother's house in Muizenburg, after which they were going to try out Gerald's new kite on the beach. Olivia and Cynthia, whose parents were long-standing friends of the Baileys, had been roped in as company for a girl who was staying with the grandmother.

The girl is French. Her name is Marie-Claude and she's the daughter of an old friend of Mrs Bailey, who in her youth studied art in Paris. Mrs Bailey is what Olivia's mother calls 'very well-connected', but she has a warm, boisterous personality, and is particularly fond of Olivia. The grandmother, on the other hand, is a dragon, who casts a cold eye on the visitors' hair and clothing, and then ignores them, while conversing graciously in French with Marie-Claude and making much of her grandsons and her other guest, whose name is Patrick. This Patrick, it seems, is a cousin of Marie-Claude's and also has relatives in South Africa who are friends of the Baileys. He's on holiday from his expensive English boarding-school and is making – like some exotic, migratory bird – his yearly visit to the Cape.

Anton (and he suspects, Olivia) feels like a village child on his best behaviour at the Manor, so it's a relief when they can finally escape the minefield of cake-forks and fragile china for the freedom of the beach. Mr Bailey piles them into his station wagon, and drives them down to Muizenburg strand, where they all help to assemble the kite. It's like nothing they've ever seen before: an enormous, magnificent, red and gold dragon, with hooked wings and trailing tail.

'It should have a name,' says Patrick, and Mr Bailey, who, like his wife, has a soft spot for Olivia, turns to her and says, 'What should Gerald call his kite, Olivia?'

But before Olivia can respond, Anton says 'Smaug'.

'I hadn't really noticed you until then,' Patrick tells him, years later, 'but when you said they should name their kite Smaug, I was amazed! A scruffy kid at some third-rate South African school who'd read The Hobbit! Hardly anyone I knew had even heard of Tolkien back then. I was blown away!'

'As was the kite,' says Anton.

He can still see it – it was his turn at last, and as a fierce gust of wind caught the kite and sent it soaring up into the air, it dragged him along. Stumbling, yelling to the others for help, all of them pelting after, grabbing at the string, to no avail. Up it went, slipping out of his grasp, unimaginably high in seconds, and racing out to sea. Gerald was in tears, the others trying awkwardly to comfort him. But it was Marie-Claude who came and put her cool smooth cheek fleetingly against

Anton's, and Patrick who said, 'Hope to see you again next year,' when they left.

The Bailey good manners forbade sulking or recriminations, but they drove home in silence. Anton, squashed miserably next to Gerald, doubted their friendship would survive, but although the kite had been lost, he was dimly aware that other bonds had been forged.

# 3

Looking back down the years, Olivia can sympathise with her father's reluctance to move, but Mrs Martin had been adamant: Cynthia and Olivia were far too young to travel all the way to and from St Anne's by train and bus each day.

Mr Martin, on the other hand, had rather enjoyed his daily, peaceful, hour-long train journey. There's no photographic record of this commute, but Olivia can picture him easily enough, in one of the First Class carriages reserved for whites. (Whites Only/Net Vir Blankes – second and third class were for coloureds, and for blacks.) First the early morning journey, the carriage full of freshly-shaven businessmen, checking documents and papers; then the late afternoon return, through the hot and gritty suburban stations, smoking and reading the evening paper as the train travels south, on down the tapering peninsula until eventually it reaches Muizenburg. This is where the ocean begins: where long stretches of wind-swept, bone-white beach unwind at the foot of the mountains. On the far side of the bay, the Hottentot's Hollands range rise out of the sea, their peaks as blue as the sky and water.

A few more stops, and Mr Martin will be home, stepping down off the platform and across the railway line that separates their village from the dunes and beach. Here, every evening after work, he swims. There's a picture of him in an ugly black woollen swimsuit, and another of the whole family eating a picnic supper on the beach. Olivia remembers these frugal evening picnics surprisingly clearly: the old rough towels wrapped around their legs to keep them warm, the flasks of tea, the hard-boiled eggs, cheese sandwiches and apples, which Cynthia eyed without enthusiasm. 'The Famous Five have potted meat and ginger beer,' she tells her sister.

Now, all these years later, Olivia surveys this childhood beach. Here in the southern hemisphere, it's autumn. The sky is blue, but the wind is biting and clouds are starting to build. Throughout most of her adult life she has returned at yearly intervals. Last year she walked arm in arm with her sister as far as the mouth of the river that flows down from the mountain. Beyond this point were quick-sands, or so her mother said; in the old days this was always the wilder, more dangerous, side of town, where an overgrown wilderness of scrub and stunted tangled trees climbed up the mountainside. It was a place they visited only on their family walks. Higher up were sandhills and caves, and people living in the bush – frozen into immobility at the sound of their voices, but there all the same. Olivia glimpsed them sometimes: silent wraith-like shapes, melting into the scrub. And no doubt there are people there still, even though the village has become a town, has grown and prospered, sprouting holiday apartments and attracting tourists, although at this time of year there are few about. In six months time it will be crowded.

For now though, she sits alone on a bench that bears her father's name: In memory of George Martin. There are plaques on most of the benches, many of them commemorating people she once knew. She watches a few hardy winter swimmers braving the surf. No-one ventures too far out, for fear of sharks, but a small red boat is heading out to sea and draws her eye along the curve of the bay towards the house with the grey roof which she always thought of as Anton's. Anton himself says he never lived there, that their house was further along: it's one of those tricks of memory that age has played on her. But there's no mistaking the Bakers' house, with its flat roof, its shutters and its terraces, descending to an arched gateway in a high white wall. As soon as her eye locates it, she remembers...

Olivia is five years old; Celeste Baker is her best friend. They lie beside each other on Celeste's parents' enormous bed, looking up at a ceiling decorated with squidgy pink nymphs and cherubs. 'My mother and father are going on the Cape to Cairo race,' says Celeste. 'They're going in the Lincoln.'

Everything about the Baker family fills Olivia with envy, from Celeste's faintly raffish parents (her mother is a tiny, elegant woman who was once a ballerina; her father deals in art) to the Italianate mansion and the gilt-framed portraits on the walls. The Lincoln, vast and sleek, is green and silver, with leather-upholstered seats; Olivia's family doesn't own a car.

When the Bakers return from this epic journey, they are full of stories. They've been through the dark interior, survived the

Congo. There are snatches of talk overheard, about the Mau Mau, their atrocities; people skinned like animals. Can this be true?

'No,' says Mrs Martin firmly, 'Of course not. And whatever terrible things are happening, I have no doubt there is wrong on both sides.'

Celeste, on the other hand, swears it's all true. 'And in Cairo a man said he'd give my father a hundred camels for my mother. He wanted to buy her for his harem.'

'What's a harem?' Olivia wants to know, but Celeste isn't sure, although she thinks it might be for special sorts of maids.

Cynthia, asked the same question, tells Olivia to go away. Cynthia is doing her homework, which given she's only eight, is not excessive, but she's already clawing her way up the academic tree. Scornful of the village school, she comes home with endless tales of its shortcomings, its brutalities. Her class teacher mispronounces words, speaks openly of 'munts' and 'kaffirs' and boys are beaten on a regular basis, sometimes in public. There's a particular ogre called Mr Van Tonder, who prowls the playground with a cane, looking for victims. Olivia, soon to start school herself, listens to her sister's stories and is for once deeply grateful that she's not a boy.

Several of the boys that Cynthia knew from school had begun to hang around the Martins' front gate recently, hoping to impress her with offerings of marbles, comics, tadpoles (all of them treated with lofty disdain) but Anton was Olivia's age. It was for her sake that he cycled past, back and forth every day, until she came out into the garden. They rarely spoke – or to be more accurate, Anton didn't speak; Olivia was rarely silent – but when she smiled at him, she saw his fair skin flush ...

*

'Olivia? Olivia Martin?'

The woman whose voice abruptly breaks the spell of childhood memories appears to be a stranger, but then something about her broad, smiling face strikes a long-forgotten chord.

'Yes – I know you, don't I?'

'Margie Lennox – from St Anne's.'

'Good heavens! Margie! It must be more than forty years!' Olivia stands, holding out her hands. 'I can't believe you recognised me!'

'Well, I've seen photos of you from time to time, and I used to hear about you when I ran into Cynthia. Of course, I haven't seen her for a while – is it true she's gone into a home?'

'Yes, her family couldn't manage any more. It's been a horrible time for everyone.'

'We were only a year apart at school.' Margie frowns. 'She can't be much over sixty?'

'Cynthia's just turned sixty-three. It doesn't seem fair, does it? But at least she's in St Cecilia's: it's as good a place as any. She seems happy enough, and the staff are wonderful.'

*Happy enough*: it's the simplest way of describing her sister's sedated state, and at least Cynthia is now washed and combed, and prevented from cutting up her underwear, or wandering down the street in the middle of the night.

'St Cecilia's is in Rosebank, isn't it?'

'Yes, quite close to Cynthia's old house. I'm staying there – I just came down today to visit childhood haunts.'

'It's such a glorious bay, isn't it? I'm always so grateful we were able to move down here when Malcolm retired. Are you in the Cape for long?'

'Just another week, then I go back to Belfast.'

'Well, I must be getting on myself, but it's been lovely to run into you.' Margie embraces her briefly. 'I've bought all your books for Owen, my grandson, by the way. He loves Paddycat!'

Olivia laughs. 'I sometimes want to strangle him, myself! But thank you, and I'm glad Owen enjoys them. Lovely to meet you again, Margie – I'll look out for you next time I'm here!'

But as she watches Margie Lennox walk away, the thought crosses her mind that she might not come back again. Her sister no longer knows her, the eleven-hour flight becomes more wearying with every passing year (and will only get worse) and although she's genuinely fond of her brother-in-law, her nieces and nephews, and one or two old friends, she finds herself increasingly reluctant to return. What she said to Anton in London is true: her home is now on the other side of the world. No, she thinks it quite likely that she won't come back – and with this in mind she decides to make one last trip, to that other place that holds so many childhood memories. Tomorrow she'll drive over the mountains to Kleinbos.

# 4

It's with a mounting sense of excitement that Olivia drives up over the pass and down into the Kleinbos Valley the next day, but anticipation starts to recede as with every mile the realisation deepens that, of course, nothing is going to be the same. The turn-off from the main road is no longer where it once was, the roads themselves are new and different – wider, smoother, faster – and the hamlet, when she finally locates it, has become a rather ugly town. There's almost nothing she recognises – a church, perhaps, an old house with a veranda half-obscured by bougainvillea – but of the dusty road leading to Mrs Fourie's hotel with its courtyard and its fig tree, there's no trace at all.

It was the first Christmas holiday the Martin family had ever spent away from home. Someone had told them about a small, cheap, private hotel in the apple-farming district of Kleinbos, where they could easily afford to spend a couple of weeks –

a peaceful, rural, under-populated district, unlike their own coastal village, which in December was always packed with summer visitors from 'up country'.

Olivia recalls these visitors: Transvaalers and Free Staters, coming down from the hinterland in their enormous cars, with their children and nursemaids packed in the back. On the beach there was always a sprinkling of pink or blue uniformed maids; watching, cajoling, drying sunburned children, but not allowed to swim themselves, because this safer end of the bay was reserved for whites. The Martins' own maid, Florence, went home to the Eastern Cape when her employers were away; Olivia's parents wouldn't have dreamt of taking her with them just to mind the children, even if they'd had a car to put her in. On this first holiday, however, the problem of transport was solved by hiring a private taxi to fetch them early in the morning and drive them over the mountains to Kleinbos: a long drive in those days, at the end of which the taxi driver was treated to a cold beer and sandwiches before pocketing his fee and driving home.

The hotel is a child's paradise: a rambling, colonial house with a long veranda overlooking the garden, and a great brass gong to summon the guests to meals. In the dining-room fans wheeze overhead, as elderly black waiters shuffle in and out with soup, then fish, then meat and vegetables, and finally, dessert. There's a frothy, sweet, milk pudding that Olivia and Cynthia both love, which is made for them by Mrs Fourie herself. (Mrs Fourie is the owner of the hotel, a huge, pale, distracted woman, dressed always in vast, faded, flowered kimonos, who rarely emerges from the kitchen.) The Martins have two adjoining rooms on the ground floor of an annex built around a courtyard where a fig tree grows. In the children's room, a marble-topped washstand with a flowered basin and a jug full of dark, earth-smelling water stands between their narrow beds. At night the top half of the door is left ajar so that they can hear the murmur of voices from across the courtyard, where their parents play bridge, or drink brandy and soda in the residents' lounge. If they look out the window in the opposite wall, they can see a vast starry sky and the black line of the forest. Olivia, whose imagination at this time is chiefly concerned with princesses and the inhabitants of enchanted woods, is bewitched by this forest; she yearns to be there after dark, to see the little winking light that will guide her to a fairy cottage; to hide behind a tree and watch the feasting and dancing that she's sure will take place in just such hidden, moonlit glades.

In years to come, she'll have recurring nightmares about this forest, but for the moment, the world of Kleinbos is sunlit and protected. The village store is an Aladdin's cave: dark and cool, with sacks of sugar, mealie meal and rice piled on the stone floor; biltong and bicycles hanging from the rafters; rolls of cheap cloth in brilliant reds, blues and greens; and jars of penny sweets. There are mules that pass early in the morning along the dusty road; long walks with their parents in the deep silence of the forests; and private games with Cynthia in the hotel grounds and buildings. They spend a lot of time spying on the residents, many of whom are retired and come from England, like wrinkled swallows, for six months of the year, thus avoiding the northern winter and substantial amounts of tax.

Kleinbos becomes a regular Christmas destination for the Martins. There are rarely any other children at the hotel, but one summer an unexpected whiff of city glamour arrives, in the person of Lilian Vermeulen. She's an unlikely person to be staying in Kleinbos – a shrewd and worldly widow who wastes no time in sizing up the other guests before seizing on Mrs Martin as the most suitable confidante. Olivia, hidden behind the sofa, listens in ...

The story is that Lilian's youngest daughter has found a job at a local school after getting engaged to a farmer she met while on holiday in Durban. He's a nice enough young man, Lilian says, but it's not the sort of match she'd hoped for. Now though, the daughter is being courted by someone else, a wealthy vineyard-owner (and a married man) which is why she, Lilian, has come down to the Cape from wherever it is that she normally roosts. 'To see how the land lies,' she says.

In the heat of the afternoon, the man who is the cause of all the trouble comes to call. He parks his fancy foreign car under the dusty eucalyptus trees, and then – unexpectedly slim and lithe – leaps like a cat up the stairs that lead to Lilian's room on the upper level. Olivia, watching from the shadows of the courtyard, is mesmerised. (Many years later she'll fall in love with a man who moves in much the same way and will remember exactly that crackle of excitement in the air; the faint, irresistible, lick of danger on her skin.)

For the time being though, a more immediate danger lurks in the cowshed, where ancient, grimy, toothless Obadiah milks the cows into a bucket. This bucket, which is not much cleaner than Obadiah, goes straight to the kitchens, and it's probably the warm, foaming milk that gives Olivia a terrible bout of dysentery. She's seven years old but has to suffer the indignity of wearing nappies, lying miserably in bed through the long, hot days, drinking glasses of cloudy water in which rice has been boiled. It's Maria who brings the rice water from the kitchens. 'Ag shame!' she says, as she puts the glass down and pats Olivia's arm. 'Arme kleintjie!' Poor little thing. Olivia understands what she says. Afrikaans is a language she's familiar with; of the many other languages spoken by the majority of people in the country, she knows only the odd word.

It's also Maria who makes their beds and takes away the laundry. She has light brown skin, and a cracked, cackling laugh, which shows that her two front teeth are missing. Once, Olivia sees her, from the empty veranda on the other side of the house, hitching up her skirt and squatting quickly to send a surprising arc of urine into one of the flowerbeds. (It doesn't occur to her that Maria isn't permitted to use the hotel lavatories, but it worries her that she seems to have no pants.) And it's because of Maria, and what happens in that year, that the sunlit world and fairy-tale forests of her imaginings become, eventually, a darker memory.

It's a hot, still morning. Creeping past the kitchens before breakfast, to spy on Major Gandy (who will be doing his exercises in his peculiar underwear) they see Maria, slumped at a table, sobbing. Olivia is worried – she's hardly ever seen an adult cry – but Cynthia grabs her wrist and pulls her round the corner, where they bump into their father who tells them to go and wash their hands, the breakfast gong will be sounding any minute.

Later, another, younger, woman comes to make their beds, and their mother tells them that Maria has gone home. It's very sad, she says, her son who was in prison in Johannesburg has died, so they must be extra kind to her when she comes back.

'Why was he in prison?' Olivia wants to know, but Mrs Martin says she isn't sure. Later though, at afternoon tea, someone else remarks on Maria's absence – she's something of a favourite with the regulars – and a young man who works for the railways and boards at the hotel, says loudly that he's sorry for Maria of course, she seems like a good girl, but as far as her son is concerned, all he can say is good riddance to bad rubbish.

'The more of these terrorists they hang, the better,' he says.

'Cynthia and Olivia,' says their mother, 'it's nearly time for the library. Go and fetch your books, please.' And finishes her tea in tight-lipped silence.

The library is one of the things Olivia loves most about these country holidays. It's run by ladies from a local Women's Institute and is open three afternoons and evenings a week. On this particular day the sun is already setting as they walk down into the village. (Their father stays behind at the hotel for a pre-dinner whisky and soda and the BBC News with Major Gandy – there is trouble brewing in the Congo, again.)

It's a beautiful evening. Olivia skips on ahead of Cynthia and her mother. She can feel the heat of the day rising from the road, but the sky is already beginning to take on the cool, greenish gleam of water. Looking up to search for the first stars, she remembers that one of them could be the Russian satellite that Cynthia told her about, the one that has a dog on board called Laika. This dog, Cynthia says, is definitely going to die – a tiny pinprick of terror, drifting inexorably away, out into the cold black night – but it's not something Olivia can bear to think about, so she focuses her attention on the hills growing shadowy and mysterious in the evening light, and concentrates on being the Princess Scheherazade. The Princess Scheherazade is never alone: at all times she is attended and adored. Graceful as a dancer, beautiful as the dawn, her silken garments and her long, long hair float out behind her as she glides on jewelled slippers through the jasmine-scented dusk.

Unfortunately, she glides right past the library, and bumps into Mr Dickey. He says, 'Hallo girly, lost your way?' and Scheherazade vanishes, flouncing off into the night. (Mr Dickey has lived in half the countries in Africa, but once the buggers start demanding independence, it's time to leave. He's an uneducated man, says their mother – this is not his fault, of course, but it's hard for Liberals to have to listen to his views.)

The library is in Miss Benjamin's old house. She lived here all the ninety years of her life, with her books and cats, and died, says Cynthia, in the enormous, echoing bathroom. This room is still in use: there's a small metal sign reading 'Lavatory' on the door, but inside it's unchanged, with its ancient rust-stained bathtub and high, meshed windows, silted up with the corpses of a million moths and beetles. Most of Miss Benjamin's books are still here too (and her ghost – Miss Le Roux has seen it twice) but the cats have long since moved out. You can sometimes see their yellow eyes, burning resentfully in the undergrowth.

The assistant at the library, who sweeps and dusts and carries books, is called Lena. She's the eldest of Maria's many daughters. They know this because Mrs Martin is the sort of woman who talks to the maids and waiters and asks about their families, but tonight, there's no sign of the silent, head-scarfed Lena; instead, Mrs Brits is on duty alone.

# 5

Mrs Brits sits, pale and solid, at her desk. If you scratched the walls of her house, Olivia suspects, you might find gingerbread underneath, and child-sized ovens in the kitchen. (She's eyeing their plump flesh even as she speaks.) She's complaining about something to Dulcie Boyd and Miss de Villiers-Grinham. The Martins join the queue and wait patiently: it doesn't do to interrupt Mrs Brits.

'Family trouble,' says Mrs Brits, and sniffs. 'Crying and carrying on all day: in the end I had to send her home, but I said to her, just you pull yourself together tomorrow, Lena my girl, and no more of this nonsense, or you'll be looking for another job!'

There's a murmur of agreement: one must be firm. But Mrs Martin takes the deep breath that warns Olivia she is going to disagree. 'But Mrs Brits,' she says, in her reasonable, educated voice, 'surely the boy who' – she glances down at her daughters – 'who died, was Lena's brother?'

Mrs Brits snorts. 'Trouble-maker, more like. I got no sympathy for him. You can't be soft, Mrs Martin – just look at what happened to Emsie!'

Silence. Emsie's fate hangs nastily in the air – whatever it was, it won't happen to Mrs Brits, that's for sure. But Olivia doesn't want to think about terrorists, or hanging, and anyway, her mother looks as if she might have more to say, so she slides her books onto the counter and takes cover in the Children's Section – an alcove crammed with bewitched maidens, ogres' castles and star-crossed younger sons. Olivia, an insatiable reader, is torn between the Yellow and the Crimson Fairy Books, and the Princess and the Goblins, which last she has already read twice, but the story of the Princess Irene, who lives in a great country full of mountains and goblins, is still her favourite. By the time she's made her choice, Mrs Brits's crony, Mrs Snyman, has arrived and the adult conversation has turned to other things. Then into a momentary silence, the name of Miss Vermeulen is dropped.

You can practically hear the ears pricking. Olivia, having eavesdropped on Lilian's conversations with her mother, knows that Miss Vermeulen (whose unlikely first name is Poppy) is Lilian's daughter. She boards with Mrs Snyman's friend, Leonie. Like the Princesses Scheherazade and Irene, Miss Vermeulen too has long, long hair. She also has a luscious bosom, and every night she climbs into an opulent car and is spirited away to unmentionable wickedness. Mrs Snyman has just discovered that the owner of the car is a wealthy gentleman farmer from the next valley who already has a wife and children – as Olivia could have told her.

'Poor lady,' says Mrs Brits. 'My heart bleeds for her.' The wife is a real Lady, what's more – an aloof, horsey Englishwoman –

unlike Miss Vermeulen, who is common, it appears, if not worse. 'A trollop,' declares Miss de Villiers-Grinham, not mincing words, and Mrs Snyman, lowering her voice (Mr Dickey is skulking in Biographies) whispers something about underwear. 'Leonie says ...' Olivia doesn't catch the rest, but the women make a hissing noise, like geese, and Mrs Brits reaches beneath the counter for the latest romance as a reward for Mrs Snyman.

In the end, Poppy Vermeulen will surprise everyone (except Olivia, who is well-versed in the ways of wicked stepmothers) by ousting her rival and moving in with her lover. Divorce and marriage will follow, with Wife No 1 forced out of the gracious gabled farmhouse into a cottage on the estate. And there she stays, within spitting distance of her rival. Olivia's mother says it's all most unfortunate, but her father laughs. He calls them Lady Horsey and Lady Hussy.

But all this is still in the future. Tonight, as they make their way back to the hotel with their books, Olivia is thinking about Lena's brother, Maria's son. She doesn't know his name, or how old he was. She knows, because her parents have told her often enough, that the laws of this country are wicked and unjust, but living as she does in a town, it's the adult workers that she sees – their children are nearly always somewhere else. Like their maid Florence's daughter, Lizzie, they live with grandparents or older relatives far away. She thinks about these other children, sleeping far from their parents in huts or shacks; children who have no books or libraries, who want their mothers. She'll ask Cynthia later about Maria's son, and what happens when someone is hanged. Or maybe not. Like the dog, Laika, it will probably turn out to be something that she's better off not knowing.

Olivia looks up. It's a luminous, magical night; the sky burns with stars, in two weeks it will be Christmas. She starts to run ahead of her mother and sister – the fleet and fearless Tiger-Lily, daughter of the Chief, gliding through the forests – then stops in her tracks because suddenly she is afraid that there are war-painted Blackfoot standing motionless in the shadows. And deep in the forest, some nameless thing, hanging from a tree and turning slowly ...

So she reaches for her mother's hand and becomes the Princess Irene instead, holding tight to her nurse as they hurry down the mountain, just one step ahead of the Goblins.

*

At a roadside farmstall, Olivia buys apple juice, and considers her next move. She's briefly tempted to press on into the interior (the mountains, at least, will surely be their old majestic selves, and she has a memory of some spectacular passes ahead that she wouldn't mind seeing one more time) but in the end she opts to drive back down towards the coast. This is the route they'd taken on one of their last family holidays in Kleinbos, when Mr Martin – a nervous but determined driver – had transported them in a borrowed car to the seaside town of Hermanus. She had wanted desperately to see a whale, but it was mid-December and the whales had long since gone, back to the Antarctic, or wherever it was that they spent the summer months.

It was also her father's great, unrequited, longing to travel (ignited during the war, according to family legend, when he'd got as far as Cairo, and gone AWOL to see the pyramids) that resulted in other more ambitious holidays. The first was when they travelled by train up into the Eastern Cape, where, from some hot and desolate junction, a smaller branch-line wound up to a little town. She has vague memories of a man with a jeep, who transported them through a violent storm, over flooded bridges and along rough and muddy tracks, right up into the Hogsback hills, to a holiday house belonging to distant cousins.

This house she remembers clearly – or thinks she does. The bedrooms were in thatched rondavels (the local name for these small circular buildings) that curved away from a central living area where a million insects fizzed and sizzled in the gaslights, where lizards flickered on the whitewashed walls, and where the enormous silence of the nights transfixed them. In the morning there was sunlight and the sound of water; raspberries and loganberries to be picked for breakfast, right outside the kitchen door; and the pleasurable terror of the outhouse, dark and spidery, with a polished wooden lavatory seat above a seemingly bottomless pit. Into this, she and Cynthia dropped endless lighted matches, which spluttered and went out long before they reached the bottom.

As the car descends towards the sea, she recalls another journey (the pinnacle of all their childhood travels) that began with a three-day cruise on a Union Castle liner up the eastern coast to Durban. They'd slept in narrow bunks, she remembers, in an inside cabin (the cheapest option) but even here they were woken each morning by a steward bringing tea and biscuits, and everyone dressed up in formal clothes for dinner. There were Officers in gleaming white, rows of deck chairs lining the rails, and organised games: deck quoits and shuffle board, sack races for the children, and someone called Uncle Arthur – Eddy? – who kept a pet snake in his pocket.

She has no recollection of their eventual disembarkation in the tropical heat of Durban, or of the old army friend of her father's who came to meet them; what she does remember is the house on a forestry plantation, high in the mountains beyond Pietermaritzburg. This house was sprawling, shabby, and seemed to float like an ark on a sea of rolling hills. She remembers the Zulu maids who sang liquid-sounding lullabies to the younger children of the family; the little, stubborn ponies she and Cynthia tried to ride; the orchard that they wandered into one morning – and she can still recall with stomach-clenching terror the moment when they realised that each and every tree around them held a huge, motionless, watching baboon. Infinitely slowly, clutching each other's hands and barely breathing, they had inched their way back towards safety.

And higher up in the mountains there were caves, with ancient Bushman paintings, said their host, so an expedition was arranged to see them.

Trekking up through the hills, they come first to a high plateau where bleached, waist-high grass ripples in the wind, and the clouds that race across the sun send shadows skimming over the ground; then there is a steep scramble up to the caves themselves. She can still see in her mind's eye the strange, elongated figures with their bows and spears – painted so long ago in shades of rust and black and sepia – that hunt their fleeing quarry across the walls of rock. And then the terrifying, precipitous, descent, made possible only because the herd-boy accompanying them as a guide sees that she is immobilised by fear. Skinny, barefoot, dressed in khaki rags – and not much older than she is – he takes her gently by the hand, and leaps back down like one of his goats, with Olivia flying behind him like a kite.

*

Many years later, standing in the heart of the Mourne Mountains with Liam McMahon, her arms resting beside his on a dry-stone wall, she watches the cloud shadows racing away.

'What are you thinking?' Liam asks.

'About a holiday I had in the mountains when I was a child.'

'In South Africa?'

She nods. 'In my memory it was idyllic: the calm before the storm.'

'Well,' he says, looking up at the gathering clouds, 'it won't be idyllic around here much longer: I think we should start on down.'

So she links her arm through his and together they pick their way carefully back down the track, two ageing survivors of their very different pasts.

# 6

'Do you need anything from the village, Anton?' Marie-Claude stands in the doorway, car keys in hand. She and Thomas – their eldest grandson – are off to investigate a newly opened sports shop, to look at some skiing equipment that Thomas has set his heart on for his birthday. Anton has always been slightly bemused by the rest of his family's enthusiasm for physical activity. He has a mild interest in cricket himself, but from their earliest years, his twin sons excelled at sport, and they are both, like their mother, accomplished skiers. Now it seems that the next generation has inherited the passion.

'I don't think so, thank you. Do we have any plans for later?'

He's only recently begun work on a new book and although he tries not to shut himself into his study when one of the grandchildren is visiting, he's grateful to Marie-Claude for ensuring that he has a few hours each day in which to work undisturbed.

Anton and Marie-Claude have been married for more than three decades. She is as cool, elegant, and capable as ever, and still teaches part-time at a local college. The twins, like their mother, are dark, clever and inscrutable. As far as Anton's concerned, it's been a highly satisfactory partnership. What Marie-Claude thinks is anyone's guess.

With fresh coffee beside him, Anton looks quickly through his emails before getting back to work. There's a communication from Patrick, who wants to know when they can join him for a week in Italy. Over the years, Patrick's villa outside Ascoli Piceno – bought with the proceeds of his second film – has become a regular holiday destination, and accordingly he makes a note to check the dates with Marie-Claude. There's also a letter from a South African friend, a publisher, remarking on the recent death of Jonathan Altman. Altman might, the friend suggests, be worth considering as a possible future subject for a biography. For a few minutes Anton sits, deep in thought, then sighs and shakes his head, before submerging himself once more in the infinitely safer world of eighteenth-century Amsterdam.

*

Some 6,000 miles away, the news of Jonathan Altman's death has finally caught up with Olivia. It's not entirely surprising that it's taken until now: when she first arrived, she'd been so preoccupied with her sister's condition and family matters, that she paid scant attention to the news, thereby missing the headlines, the photographs, the obituaries. The press has since moved on to other things – another presidential scandal, an accident claiming dozens of lives, trouble in Zimbabwe – so it's only when she picks up a local paper in Hermanus, that she sees, on an inner page, a tribute: Jonathan Altman, Man of Conscience.

There's a moment of intense shock, then her eye skims over the article. Words jump out: internationally respected lawyer, human rights, Sharpeville, the ANC, Mandela – but it's the personal details she's after, and there they are: married twice, his second wife from an old Hermanus family, hence the local tribute. Survived by his daughter, Rebecca, and his son, David.

'That's the Altmans' house,' Celeste Baker had said, all those years ago.

'Who are the Altmans?'

'Jonathan Altman. You know – that boy who's going out with Cynthia's friend. He's a law student.'

'Oh yes, him,' says Olivia. 'He's very good-looking.'

Celeste and Olivia are still considered too young to be going out with anyone, but the affairs of Cynthia and her friends are a topic of intense speculation.

'The Altmans are Jewish,' Celeste informs her. 'That's why they're so rich.'

'How do you know them?'

'I've been to their house with my father. They've got a lot of paintings.'

Olivia has promised Florence that she and Celeste, whose mother has driven up to town and dropped her off for the day, are just going to the Greek shop on the corner to buy sweets, but they've taken the long way round in order to walk past the high walls and imposing houses of the Altman's neighbourhood. Celeste still lives in their childhood village down the coast, but the Martins, when they moved to Cape Town, had, for reasons of economy and convenience, rented an apartment in an old-fashioned block called Balmoral.

As flats go, it's not bad: reasonably spacious, with two balconies that overlook the city. In hot weather, the glass doors onto these balconies are usually left open – even at night. (These are the days before electric fences and panic buttons, when there are no non-whites on the streets after dark – unless they're resident domestic servants, with the papers to prove it.) Unfortunately, Cynthia and Olivia still have to share a bedroom, which makes it hard to have friends to stay, but the novelty of living in a flat at the foot of Table Mountain is some compensation. And in the school holidays Celeste comes up to visit Olivia, and Olivia, rather more often, goes down to stay with Celeste.

'Olivia, darling!' Mrs Baker embraces her, then holds her at arm's length to scrutinise her. 'How beautiful you've become!'

This is balm to Olivia's ears: usually it's Cynthia who is described as beautiful.

'And do you like your new school? Are you still doing ballet?'

The answer to both these questions is no – Olivia has recently abandoned her hopes of becoming a ballerina, and joined the school's dramatic society instead, where she has slightly more chance of shining; Celeste, on the other hand, has inherited her mother's talent, and is a dancer of promise. But Mrs Baker barely pauses. 'My goodness, look at the time! I must fly. Enjoy your day, my darlings!' And blowing kisses she departs, leaving Olivia and Celeste in the care of the maid, and free to amuse themselves as they see fit.

What they most enjoy is experimenting with Mrs Baker's cosmetics (her dressing table holds a feast of imported lipsticks, eye shadows, pencils) then choosing costumes from the dressing-up chest in Celeste's room and acting out plays or ballets. These performances take place in the shadowy grandeur of the sitting room, to the music of Tchaikovsky and Prokofiev, on the Bakers' enormous, stereo record-player. Just recently though, they've started dancing to other records (surreptitiously taken from Celeste's older sister's room) and the exciting new music of Buddy Holly, Elvis Presley.

Celeste, who is a kind-hearted girl, pretends to envy Olivia's new city life and flat, but they both know that the Bakers' lifestyle is infinitely more desirable. Inevitably, Olivia goes back home from these visits feeling deeply dissatisfied – and slightly guilty, because one of the many things she enjoys about staying with the Bakers is the complete absence of any political talk.

Both Mr and Mrs Martin are long-standing members of the beleaguered Liberal Party: there are occasional meetings in their flat, and Mrs Martin has joined the women's opposition movement, the Black Sash. For the most part the members of this organisation are decent, white, middle-class matrons who stand silently outside Parliament, or on the steps of the Cathedral, wearing the black sash that signifies mourning for their country. Holding placards that denounce whatever wicked bit of legislation is about to be passed – *We Stand for Human Rights. Say NO to Pass Laws* – they are often loudly reviled, and occasionally spat on; but the Martins and their friends, despite the times, are sustained by a sense of righteous purpose, and an exhilarating belief that a great change is coming.

Olivia believes this too; she's just not sure what sort of change it's going to be. Living here, on the slopes of the great mountain, everything feels fiercer, more spectacular. The sky burns blue or churns with enormous clouds; wind, fire, and rain sweep in cycles through the mountains, and the famous tablecloth of cloud rolls down above them like a breaking wave.

It's soon after Sharpeville that she begins to dream of another wave, a gigantic tsunami crashing over Kloof Nek – the gap between the right-hand flank of Table Mountain and the rising cone of Lion's Head – and pouring down onto the unsuspecting city. In her dream the wave sweeps everything away in one monstrous, swirling tide of water, and Cape Town, like Atlantis, is gone. This particular dream retains its power to haunt her throughout her life: even years later, in the midday city heat, when she raises her eyes to that gap in the encircling mountains, she feels a frisson of fear that she'll see a great silent wave, curling up into the sky.

Sharpeville. She hears about it first from her mother, who is distraught. There is no television in South Africa, so there are no live pictures, and the radio is state-controlled, but in the end, nothing can stop the horror of the story getting out: which is that scores of men, women and children have been shot down by the police at a peaceful, unarmed protest – many of them in the back, as they tried to flee.

Olivia feels sick with guilt and fear. It's her tribe that has done this, after all, and retribution is sure to follow – how can all those other wronged millions not now rise up and kill the white oppressors in their beds? Quite apart from her long-standing fear that the Security Forces will come to arrest her parents for their political activities (for some time now, her father has had a packed suitcase waiting in the hall, against this eventuality) Olivia's over-active imagination has always made her afraid: of the dark, of supernatural forces, of murderers. Now she lies in bed at night listening for the tramp of other feet, for the screams, the battering down of doors. She has no hope that her father and mother's commitment to the Anti-Apartheid movement will protect them: why should anyone believe they're not like all the others? Her parents will almost certainly be killed, and even if she and Cynthia hide under their beds, she knows they'll be found and dragged out to their deaths.

A different type of fear attaches to the playing fields of St Anne's. The grounds of St Anne's are suitably imposing, and the playing fields afford extensive views of the mountain. In years to come, Olivia will sometimes think that to be swept away in an apocalyptic flood might be preferable to one more hockey session in the stinging winter cold; or one more length of painful, floundering crawl in the hostile chlorinated waters of the school swimming-pool. She hates the communal concrete changing-rooms, the hideous, unflattering uniform they're forced to wear, and she especially loathes the games mistress, who returns her sentiments with interest – and with the particular contempt that she reserves for malingerers and girls with No Team Spirit.

Her new classmates also regard her with suspicion – and Elizabeth Viljoen is her principal foe. Elizabeth is shiny with health and promise. Like a well-groomed pony (and unlike Olivia) she has snow-white socks, and her hair and teeth gleam. She is both clever and ambitious, and on the look-out for dissidents and non-conformists.

'What school did you go to before this one?' A little circle of girls has surrounded Olivia at break-time, and Elizabeth has appointed herself Chief Inquisitor. She raises one eyebrow at the reply: not a private school, evidently.

'And where do you live now?' Elizabeth appears to be showing a kindly interest, but in reality is probing for weak spots.

'Across the road, in Balmoral.' Realising as she says it that this is a mistake.

'My auntie used to live in Balmoral,' a girl called Susan says. 'She had quite a nice flat.'

Susan is Elizabeth's best friend. She is small and anxious, and easily quelled by Elizabeth, who gives her a withering look and says, 'Flats are all right for *single* people, Susan, not for families.' And Olivia knows, without having to be told, that Elizabeth will turn out to live in Constantia or Bishopscourt, in a house surrounded by manicured lawns and with an abundance of pink-uniformed maids to tend to the Viljoen family's every need; that her parents will own at least two cars – a Mercedes for her father, probably, and a smart little run-about for her mother. The Martins, of course, have no car at all, but she's not going to admit to this shameful fact until she's forced to.

A girl called Vanessa du Toit rolls her eyes behind Elizabeth's back, and smiles at Olivia in quite a friendly way. Unfortunately, Vanessa du Toit already has a best friend called Terry, and this is the problem: everyone else has a best friend. Even the dullest and least attractive girl is paired with another. There is slow, bespectacled Jessie, mind you, who has no best friend – indeed, no friend at all – but Olivia can see that to align herself with

Jessie would be to commit social suicide, and things are bad enough already.

Quite apart from her parents' political beliefs, Olivia's family is poor by the standards of most of her classmates, and to help with their daughters' school fees, Mrs Martin has taken a secretarial job. Both she and her husband now walk to work in the mornings: a further sign of eccentricity in the eyes of most of their neighbours, although in Mr Martin's eyes it's not just an economy, but a healthy, if less enjoyable, alternative to the daily swim he used to enjoy.

As always, Olivia takes refuge from daily life in books. To the tales of princesses in castles, and stories of magical adventures, she now adds myths and legends and historical novels, and as she moves up into the middle school, she makes a few friends and, although she's no Cynthia and wins no prizes, she has some modest success. Her artwork is regularly printed in the school magazine; she even becomes, to her own surprise, an accepted member of the dramatic society. Her mother encourages her, likes to discuss which university she will apply to after Matriculation; Olivia, on the other hand, already knows that none of this is going to last.

'I suppose it's to be expected at her age …' Mrs Martin, until now preoccupied with her busy life and political activities, and in no way prepared for teenage rebellion, has finally begun to have misgivings, which she eventually confides to her best friend, Vera.

'I must say, we had nothing like this with Cynthia. Olivia really has become very difficult.'

'Boys?' asks Vera.

'Oh no!' Mrs Martin is shocked. 'Nothing like that! But she's started to say school's a waste of time; she wants unsuitable clothes, make-up – I even caught her wearing lipstick, at fourteen! And the latest thing is, she's refusing to go to church.'

'Oh, you can't have that,' says Vera. 'I would insist, if I were you. It's good discipline, if nothing else.'

So church attendance on Sundays remains compulsory, and make-up and clothing are fought over every inch of the way. At school things get worse: her work deteriorates, her reports are disappointing, and she's in constant trouble for breaching the multitudinous regulations that govern uniform and behaviour. Olivia herself sometimes feels she'll die of fury and boredom before she can escape. Her parents are bewildered: they simply can't understand how an intelligent young woman can fail to make the most of the education and opportunities that are given to so few in their country.

What Olivia wants, of course, is excitement, admiration and freedom from constraint; anything that will deliver her from the dreary horrors of adolescence and turn her into someone new. She wants to throw herself into Life – to be consumed by it. What she craves most of all is Love.

# 7

Until the Martins moved away, Anton had never had any reason to imagine life without Olivia. He loved her. It didn't matter that they hardly spoke to each other – when they were older, he knew they would get married; and as long as he could ride past her house on his bicycle every day (a knight on his horse, attendant on his lady) and see her in the garden with her sister, all was well. And then, just like that, the garden was empty and Olivia was gone, leaving Anton bereft. (Admittedly Cape Town was only an hour away by train, but from his perspective, it might as well have been another country.)

'What's the matter with the boy?' Even Mr de Waal had noticed the change in his son, but his mother, having seen the way the wind was blowing, quickly arranged for him to spend the rest of the holidays with cousins of his fathers on their farm near Swellendam. And although, at first, the prospect of being packed off to this distant, rural outpost seemed to Anton like further punishment, in the end, the visit turned out to be surprisingly successful – indeed, the first of many.

He remembers the brilliant clarity of those early mornings on the farm; the long walks with Cousin Manus (three years older) and the family dogs; the brackish waters of the dam where they swam each day – and the unexpected pleasure of being teased and admired by Manus's sisters, Anna and Reinette, and Anna's friend Marlene.

In the year that Manus turned eighteen, the direction of travel was reversed, and Manus, Anna and Marlene all came down to the Cape to spend two weeks with the De Waals. The day after they arrived, his mother made them a picnic supper to take to the beach in the late afternoon, and it was there, in the privacy of the sand dunes, that he dared to put his arms around the plump and pliant body of Marlene and press his lips to hers. It was his first kiss. She smacked his hand away sharply when he tried to investigate the breasts encased in her old-fashioned floral swimsuit, but she did it good-humouredly, and at least it was a start.

In the meantime, another family had moved into the Martins' old house, and Anton had struck up a friendship with their son, a boy called Jan. Jan, as luck would have it, was a kindred spirit, and like Anton, blessed with a bicycle. Together they made the most of the considerable freedom allowed at the time – to boys – to cycle, to swim, and at weekends to camp by themselves in their gardens or in a neighbour's field. They poured over their collections (comics, stamps and model planes) pooled their knowledge of girls (limited) and discussed their ambitions (vague but wide-ranging). As they grew older, their determination to get away from their small town – and indeed, their country – only increased. They both knew military service was inevitable: unlike their more fortunate fellows at private schools (who were widely believed by the less privileged to be granted exemption on the flimsiest of grounds) boys from government schools rarely managed to avoid conscription. Afterwards, though, they both intended to go on to university, and with this in mind they applied themselves fairly diligently to their studies. Looking back, Anton remembers it as a largely pleasant and uneventful childhood and adolescence; Olivia's, unsurprisingly, turns out to have been a lot more turbulent.

*

In the year that she turned fifteen, Olivia's growing sense of dissatisfaction was made worse by the fact that Celeste and her family were away, spending the summer in Europe. Postcards arrived from Rome, from Paris, and from the heart of the Swinging 60s: London. To Olivia, lying on her bed and listening to Top of the Pops on Cynthia's radio (Roy Orbison was at No 1 with Pretty Woman) life seemed grossly unfair. Then the phone in the hall rang, and it was one of her classmates, inviting her to a birthday party ...

The house is huge. Even Cynthia's well-to-do boyfriend Simon, who has volunteered to drop Olivia off, is impressed by the oak-lined drive, the gabled façade. There's a wide, high-ceilinged hallway leading to the rear of the house, where French windows open out onto immaculate gardens, and where a room has been cleared for the twenty or so girls to dance (with each other) to the music of the Beatles, the Byrds, the Rolling Stones. An older brother of the birthday girl is also present; he presides over the record-player and pours soft drinks, and he's brought along a friend of his own for company. It's this friend who, later in the evening, persuades Olivia out into the shadowy garden and onto a canopied swinging seat – or perhaps it's she who lures him out: who knows? At any rate, she no longer remembers anything about the boy, but she can recall in perfect detail her rose-pink dress, with its tight waist and full skirt, and the row of tiny buttons on the bodice, with which the boy inexpertly fumbles as he kisses her. It's her first real kiss, but what she's most gleefully conscious of is that she's stolen a march on all her school-friends – particularly Elizabeth Viljoen. Elizabeth stands with her cronies, seething (Olivia hopes) with outrage and envy as they peer, scandalised, from the windows, while she, Olivia, gets off with the only available male. (The brother, in the role of chaperone, is hors de combat for the evening.)

This incident confirms the general suspicion that Olivia is not, after all, a Nice Girl.

Niceness is, at this time, an obsession. Endless break-time conversations and whispered discussions at night revolve around the things that nice girls should and shouldn't do. Boys don't have to be nice because they have wild oats to sow (in bad girls, presumably) but they are expected to be able to recognise the nice girls, and to respect them accordingly. Nice girls are popular: like Cynthia, they are invited to school dances, and are taken out to dinner and to the cinema – the 'bioscope' – for which everyone dresses up, in suits and cocktail frocks. After a suitable period of courtship, older boys and girls may drive to the seafront, or along the lower slopes of the mountain, and park for a while. It's acceptable for a girl to let a boy kiss her, to allow a certain amount of above-the-waist intimacy, but anything further will lead, almost certainly, to disaster. To loss of respect and, worst fear of all, to pregnancy, which is when the whole world will come crashing down around your ears.

'Olivia, stop clicking that bloody pen and finish your homework! You've been staring out the window for hours.'

Olivia, who has spent the last two weeks constructing various scenarios to explain the failure of the boy who kissed her at the party to get in touch, glares at her sister. The shared bedroom with its two desks is not an ideal arrangement. At one desk Cynthia, now a first year medical student, works diligently, night after night; at the other, Olivia spends most of her time doodling, and staring out at a view of the city – a view which never fails to fill her with a wild longing to get away. To run out into the dark and lose herself in the music, the dancing, the *life* that she knows is going on somewhere out there.

'It's all right for you,' says Olivia, 'you were always good at Maths and History and horrible, boring Biology. I'm no good at anything except English and Art.'

'You'd be better at everything if you worked harder,' her sister says. 'Like me.'

'You're just a freak!' Olivia glares at her. 'A machine. Work, work, work all the time – it isn't natural.'

'The reason I worked at school,' says Cynthia, 'was so that I could get a First Class Matric and go to Medical School. And when I'm a doctor I'll have enough money to buy a big house and my eldest daughter won't have to share a room with her bloody younger sister.'

Cynthia, at eighteen, is already being courted by several suitable young men, including the superior Simon; Olivia, three years younger, is still thought far too young to have a boyfriend. But it's not much more than a year later that she loses her virginity on a beach one night, to a friend of the brother of another of her classmates. It's essentially an act of defiance – if boys are allowed to do what they want, why shouldn't she? – not that she's entirely sure that this is what she wants, but at a certain point it seems a bit late to object.

Neither she nor the boy were prepared for what happened, and for a brief period she's afraid she might be pregnant. Once this proves not to be the case, she does at least have the sense to persuade her mother to arrange an appointment with their family doctor, ostensibly to advise what to do about her occasional acne, but in reality to persuade Dr Long to prescribe the new, miraculous, contraceptive pill, about which everyone (including her mother) is talking, and which – luckily for Olivia – is thought to be good for skin problems.

Dr Long is a good, old-fashioned, family doctor. He's happy to make home visits, particularly in the early evening, when a glass of sherry is likely to be offered, but Olivia goes to his surgery. She's reasonably certain he'll do as she asks – and more importantly, not tell her mother – because in recent years his avuncular fondness for her has progressed to his putting an arm around her shoulders as he escorts her to the door at the end of a consultation, and occasionally patting her bottom. 'Olivia, Olivia,' he always says, shaking his head mournfully, paternally. 'What *are* we going to do with you?' Then he puts both arms around her and hugs her silently against his paunch. There doesn't seem to be anything particularly sexual in these exchanges, but they appear to give him some pleasure, or possibly comfort, and although they make Olivia feel uncomfortable, they are also her insurance that her secrets will stay safe.

She's fully aware that she's embarking on a risky journey, that she's stepping across the threshold of a dangerous world, but she also knows she's going to let the door slam shut behind her. So, in the mornings she goes to school, where she works with less and less enthusiasm, while at night she leads her other life – and there's no shortage of excitement now, because these are changing, hazardous, times. Years later, she looks back on this period and is aghast at the risks she took, staying out time and again until the early hours of the morning; dancing, drinking and occasionally falling into bed with men she barely knew. She doesn't find love, but she does discover the excitement of sexual power, of being considered original, unconventional. There are parties in forbidden areas of the city, intense conversations entered into with strangers in houses she would never have found by day, and in her final year at school, she meets the two young men who will introduce her to so much more.

# 8

The party is at Celeste Baker's house. A famous ballerina is in town, and the Bakers have invited some of their arty friends to meet her. Celeste's elder sister Nicole has been allowed to ask a few friends from university, and Olivia has been invited down for the weekend as company for Celeste. She makes herself useful (and noticeable) by offering to hand round canapés and savouries, gradually working her way from the ballerina (beautiful but chilly) to the older guests, then to the younger crowd, and finally to the two young men – one dark, one fair – who have been standing to one side, deep in conversation, but who have been watching her, she knows, just as she has been watching them.

'Hello,' says the shorter one. He reaches for a vol au vent. 'I'm Jason, and this is Grant.'

Jason is handsome, fair-haired, smiling; Grant is dark and saturnine. They're older than the boys she usually meets, graduates – or about to graduate – and they are at Cape Town's cutting intellectual and unconventional edge, or so they think. In their early twenties, they're full of charm and dangerous theories; the newest of new brooms, intent on sweeping aside all the old, outworn, morality. They certainly charm Olivia, and she, in turn, is encouraged to entertain them with increasingly outrageous stories about St Anne's.

'I can't believe you're still at school,' Jason shakes his head in disbelief. 'We thought you must be a very upmarket waitress, or else one of Nicole's friends.'

'It's my last year,' Olivia replies, 'thank God.'

'And then? What do you want to do?'

'I don't know. I haven't decided yet.'

'Don't worry,' says Grant, 'we can help you. We're good at careers advice, aren't we Jason?' He draws slowly on his cigarette as he considers her. 'You've got a very expressive face. The stage, perhaps – or cinema? You look a bit like Jeanne Moreau, you know.'

(Luckily, Olivia knows who Jeanne Moreau is. She's seen pictures of the French film star in copies of Paris Match. Her French teacher is a clever woman who has arranged a subscription to this glamorous magazine: she knows her pupils are far more like to struggle to translate the captions if they concern the lives of the rich and famous.)

Grant and Jason are intellectuals. Their conversation is littered with heady references to Foucault, Sartre, Solzhenitsyn – names she tucks away for later investigation in the public library. They are also aspiring writers, working on avant-garde novels, and they plan to move to London as soon as they can – or possibly Ireland – and take the literary world by storm. In the meantime, they draw Olivia into their lives; they discuss their work and read daring passages to her in their flat, where she's soon a regular visitor. She's their pet, their new toy – their naughty schoolgirl. She bunks off sport, Debating Society – even Drama – in order to meet them after school and be taken to unsuitable places, where they initiate her into the pleasures of cannabis, and show her off to their friends, who applaud her rebelliousness, her refusal to accept conventional constraints. It's 1967, after all, and the waves of the swinging sixties have rippled even as far as Cape Town.

It's Grant that Olivia falls in love with and does her best to impress. (Secretly, she dreams of marrying him, even though she'd sooner die than admit to such bourgeois longings.) He, on the other hand – although he feels genuine affection for her – chiefly enjoys encouraging her wilfulness: for him, it's all part of a highly amusing game, and Olivia is the victim of her own success at playing it. Flattered, intoxicated by this picture of herself as a fearless poster-girl for the cultural and sexual revolution, she abandons herself to the new freedoms, and only realises years later how little freedom she really had – indeed, how much freer she might have been under the old dispensations.

Stormy confrontations with parents and teachers inevitably became more frequent, but Olivia – unmoved by the threats and prohibitions, by the tears and lamentations of her mother – simply kicked against convention all the harder. She saw herself as an adventurer, a free spirit; the heroine (possibly doomed) of her own screenplay. She was Camille, Juliet, Scarlet O'Hara ...

Unfortunately, she was also still Olivia Martin, and her examinations loomed, but before then there was the night of the Matric Dance – the social highlight, supposedly, of her entire school career.

Olivia, while pretending to scoff at the whole idea, secretly intends to outshine everyone there. To this end she's called a truce with her mother and persuaded her to make a sophisticated dress: an elegant, floor-length sheath of satin, with matching shoes and elbow-length gloves.

On the night of the dance, with her hair swept up in a chignon, pale pearly lips, and eyes outlined in black (the Audrey Hepburn look is what she's after) she makes her entrance into her parents' sitting room.

Her mother and father are there, with a few of their activist friends; there are half-eaten sandwiches, coffee-cups, piles of paper on every surface. Also present is a young black man called Thabo, and another man who is his friend or relative. Thabo is small, quiet, self-possessed, and like her, only seventeen. Unlike her, he's about to spend his last night in South Africa. He will stay overnight (illegally) in a safe house, to be sure of catching the plane the next day that will take him to England, where he's won a scholarship to a university somewhere in the cold, wet depths of that unknown country. His own home is in a distant rural district – he has a widowed mother, several siblings, the usual background of poverty and deprivation. He's never been to Cape Town before, never been on a plane, and he'll leave on an Exit Permit which means that he doesn't know when, if ever, he'll be allowed to return. His friend is called Joseph. He's a year or two older, thin-faced, with a scar that runs down his left cheek. He is here to give Thabo moral support; after tomorrow he'll disappear back into his dangerous, shadowy world.

There's a brief lull in the conversation when she enters the room, followed by several gratifying looks and comments, but it's Thabo who stands, and bows. 'I did not know your daughter was so beautiful,' he says to her father. Then he presses his hand to his heart. 'Tonight, you are a Princess.'

For a moment she's afraid that she'll cry. She is at one and the same time delighted with the compliment and pierced with sadness by the knowledge of his coming exile – as well as being deeply ashamed of the difference in their lives. Then Grant arrives with an orchid to pin to her dress (the orchid is this season's most sophisticated and desirable corsage) and she leaves the flat in a flurry of excited anticipation.

She never sees Thabo again, but years later she learns that he completed his studies successfully and stayed on in England. Whether he eventually returned to South Africa, her informant cannot say, although he imagines that he did. Unexpectedly, she finds herself filled with sorrow, and with the fierce hope that he did go back, and that he has been happy. The fate of his friend Joseph is something she knows only too well.

# 9

The Matric dance. She remembers the school hall (also the gym) being ineffectually disguised for the night with a painted backdrop on the stage. A moonlit sea and a castle? Something like that. The gym equipment is partially hidden under velvet curtains borrowed from Elizabeth Viljoen's family; a large gilt-framed mirror (also borrowed) hangs from the climbing bars, balloons and paper lanterns are suspended from the ceiling, and a row of wooden chairs lines the rear wall for the teachers.

The staff – all women, few of them young – are wearing a startling variety of evening dress, the overall impression being that they've raided some ancient dressing-up box. Their pupils, on the other hand, are resplendent in the latest fashions. They are dewy, pampered, and busy sizing up each other's partners ...

The greatest shame was to be accompanied by your brother, or some other family member, dredged up because no-one else could be found – any awkward, spotty boy was better than that. The most admired girls were partnered by handsome older boys in dinner jackets; they wore orchids and their mother's earrings and one or two had even had their hair professionally done. Grant, Olivia was gratified to discover, inspired ferocious envy, and together they made a sufficiently glamorous and sophisticated-looking couple to put several noses out of joint – and to cause the Headmistress to eye them with misgiving. (As well she might, because halfway through the night they slipped out through the door and crept along the cloisters to the chapel, where, beneath the disapproving gaze of St Anne, they shared a companionable joint.)

*

When Olivia's examination results finally arrive, she is found – unsurprisingly – to have failed her Matriculation. Uproar ensues; but with a bit of string-pulling by her art teacher, and on the strength of a fairly flimsy portfolio of work, she manages in the end to scrape into the University's School of Art. And it's there, at the start of her first term, that she re-encounters Anton.

He'd arrived on the little bus that shuttled students between the main campus and the School of Art and was waiting with his group outside the room where their History of Art lecture was scheduled to begin. A girl called Jenny, in whom he was vaguely interested, was busy telling him about her recent holiday in Rhodesia – a country he was hoping to visit soon himself – when something behind him caught her eye and she broke off with a small laugh.

'Don't look now, but I think we're about to be joined by some genuine art students!'

Turning, Anton sees coming towards them two boys and

a girl. All three are dressed in black and have long untidy hair, which in the girl's case is mostly piled up at the back of her head. Silver hoops hang from her ears, her eyes are huge dark smudges, her lips are pale, and she's smoking a pungent-smelling cigarette. Despite the transformation, he knows her at once. It's Olivia.

She walks past without noticing him, but at the end of the lecture he contrives to hold the door open for her, and when she glances at him, he says, 'Olivia?'

'Yes? Oh, my goodness!' The studied coolness drops away and that extraordinary smile lights up her face. 'It's ...?'

'Anton de Waal,' he supplies. 'I used to live a few streets away from you.'

'Of course, I remember you! And you were at primary school with me, we were in the same class. So, what are you doing here? Is this your first year?'

'Yes. I've managed to defer my military service. I'm doing History, and History of Art, so I'll be coming over here once or twice a week.'

Her friends are waiting for her; they're going for coffee in a café nearby. 'Come with us,' she says, so he does, ignoring Jenny's disapproving look, and the bus waiting to take him back to other lectures.

The café is full of art students. He feels out of place with his short hair and clean sweater, but Olivia draws him in: 'This is Anton, my old school-friend.'

'What, you went to St Anne's?' asks one of the girls, in mock surprise.

Olivia throws back her head and laughs. 'My *primary* school Suzette – but I wasn't there for very long.'

'She was like a comet flashing through our skies,' says Anton. 'We were all in love with Olivia.' And wonders which of them is in love with her now.

Olivia remembers their encounter slightly differently.

Art school appeals to her mainly because she can re-invent herself as a student, and it gives her something to do when Grant and Jason unexpectedly achieve their ambitions and decamp to London after all. She wears black tights and roll-neck sweaters, and smokes Gitanes, but does very little actual work. Mostly she is discovering Life, in the course of which she makes a lot of strange and unsuitable friends. She also runs into Anton de Waal, a boy she remembers from her primary school, who turns up for History of Art lectures. She likes him, but there's something a bit intimidating about his intelligence, his slightly fastidious reserve: she feels more than usually frivolous in his company. She remembers a day when he joined a group of her friends for coffee, and she said, 'I can't stay long, I've got to go and take off my clothes for Dracula.' When it was explained to him that Dracula was their name for one of their lecturers (a well-known Cape Town artist) and that Olivia was his latest model, Anton's disapproval was palpable.

Dracula (rumoured to be a Count) has brooding, satanic looks and is famous for his nudes. His latest portrait of Olivia is already greatly admired. It depicts her lying sprawled on an old, intricately-patterned kilim – the scene of who knows how many earlier couplings with his models, because he takes it for granted that Olivia will join him there at the end of each session for twenty minutes of mutual abandonment before he goes home to the current Mrs Dracula.

Olivia, looking back, can't really remember what she felt. Probably a mixture of curiosity and lust – Dracula was, after all, strangely magnetic. Who knows? At any rate, she was paid very little for her time, although he did part with the odd preliminary sketch, which he rather grudgingly signed. Keep them safe, he instructed, they will make you money one day. And they might well have done, if she hadn't left them in her mother's safekeeping: by the time she got round to asking for them back, Mrs Martin could no longer remember what had happened to them, although Olivia strongly suspects they were burned.

*

Decades later, when Liam McMahon came so unexpectedly into her life, the painting was one of the first things he noticed in her workroom.

'That's lovely!' He bent closer to look at the signature. 'I don't recognise the name.'

'Andries du Plessis,' said Olivia. 'We used to call him Dracula. I was his model.'

'Really?' They stood for a while in silence, contemplating the painting. It wasn't very big, perhaps thirty by forty centimetres, and showed a young girl, lying naked on a vivid rug; the intense blues, reds and golds of the fabric framed the creamy glow of her skin, the dark hair spread out like a fan.

'It reminds me of a Klimt. How old were you when it was painted?'

'Seventeen or eighteen. I was an art student, he was one of our lecturers.'

'Posing naked for a teacher?' – he shook his head and laughed – 'How times have changed!'

'I think I felt quite honoured. He is – was – highly-regarded in South Africa.'

'And he gave this to you?'

'Oh no, he would never have parted with a valuable painting, but someone I knew bought it, and years later it came back to me.'

Liam studied her face. 'Someone you loved?'

'Oh yes.'

There are other paintings of Olivia in existence, and some hang far from home – a larger version of the same picture hangs in a loft apartment in New York, others in Australia and Europe – but as Dracula never named his models (most probably, Olivia suspects, because he couldn't remember what they were called) there is nothing to connect her now with these youthful, sensual nudes.

Olivia herself left home shortly after she turned eighteen, abandoning her place at art school in favour of a job as an artist's model at another local college. The wages from this, together with a small allowance from her father, and what she earned modelling for Dracula and others, just about covered the rent on a tiny upstairs room in a dilapidated house in the Tamboerskloof district of the city. Her parents, although anxious and unhappy, were unable to stop her moving out – and in the end, life without Olivia proved so much less of a strain that they had to admit to a certain degree of relief. Besides, Cynthia had recently announced her engagement to Simon, a young man so eligible, so suitable in every possible way, that Mrs Martin couldn't help feeling grateful that her wayward younger daughter had, for the time being at least, removed herself from the family orbit.

*

Olivia is drying her hair in front of a panel of speckled mirror set into the door of an ugly wardrobe, and sees her rented room reflected in the glass. Apart from the wardrobe, she has a bed, a spindly table and chair, a thin piece of carpet and a bird's eye view of the city and the bay from a small window set into the sloping roof. To be honest, she's as much appalled as excited by the way she has precipitated herself out into the world on her own; but the room is cheap, and most importantly, she has somewhere of her own at last; a room, however shabby, where she can finally do exactly as she pleases.

At the moment she's waiting for Damien, her latest boyfriend. Damien is English. He's one of the new wave of young travellers suddenly buccaneering round the globe, and he has both the looks and glamour of a fallen angel. Olivia doesn't know if she's in love, but she very much wants to be, and she craves the excitement that hangs around Damien like a whiff of brimstone. Together they roam the city at night, gravitating to the area known as District Six, where danger is never far away, and where they buy handfuls of pills in rooms full of dagga-smoke and jazz; where by day the washing hangs from peeling balconies and the streets are of full of raucous life. (Until the houses are all bulldozed and the mixed-race residents moved far away to the dusty, catastrophic wastes of Mitchell's Plain.) They go to occasional parties in luxurious, suburban houses, and to hotels where, for the price of a drink, they can dance until the band goes home; and more often than not they go down to the docks in the early hours of the morning, to the Harbour Café, where all the strange human flotsam and jetsam of Cape Town washes up; where fights break out, women cry, and people are stabbed. And somewhere out across the black night water, the future leader of the country lies imprisoned on Robben Island.

Olivia and Damien creep back before dawn, past the closed doors of the four other tenants and her landlords, whose names she has now forgotten. Mr & Mrs Nameless, pale, plump, and uneasy, who live with their thin, silent children on the ground floor of the house and rent out the rooms on the floors above. Their most respectable tenant is German Gunther, who works long hours and is saving all his money to buy a car; then there is the man who drinks, who shakes and swears and cries out at night in the room next door to Olivia's, and the mouse-like woman who only ever speaks to Mrs Nameless. There is also the person who is never seen at all, whose door clicks shut as Olivia climbs the stairs.

She has plenty of friends these days. She can't afford to be a student any longer, but she keeps in touch with old friends from art school, and she's made new friends at the college where she now works as an artist's model, and where she is in great demand for life-drawing classes. She's a particular favourite with the ladies' sculpture class, whose members immortalise her most often as a simpering stone nymph to set beside their ornamental fishponds. She also works for several well-known painters and sculptors apart from Dracula. There's the man who famously paints her lying beside a stuffed lion; and most eminent of all, the elderly, one-time pupil of Matisse, whose portrait of her (a contorted odalisque with bluish skin) hangs for many years in the National Gallery.

All this is presented to her friends as a life of heady, devil-may-care glamour: she's a muse, a free spirit, an inspiration to creative genius – and if there are times when she has trouble maintaining this illusion, she keeps them to herself. She also manages to disguise any distress she feels when Damien eventually takes off to join the hippy trail to India, and anyway, his place is taken soon enough by Marcus, a young Swede who works for a shipping line. He, in turn, is replaced by a boy who will die fighting for Rhodesia. For all of them Olivia feels affection, and physical attraction, but not, sadly, the overpowering love she'd hoped to find. She's beginning to suspect that for her, at least, it doesn't exist.

Then, one night, she has a chance encounter on the steps of a house where a party is being held. It's a hot summer's evening, she's barefoot and high, gazing up at the great dark sky, adrift. The man, a young Jewish lawyer, whom she knows by sight, is leaving the house alone, and stops to ask her what she's thinking about. She replies, for no reason at all, 'Jelly babies', and he laughs, before moving on lightly down the steps.

Olivia watches him go with some regret. She knows who he is, has seen him at other parties, and been attracted not just by his looks, but by his air of focused, watchful, energy. Ten, fifteen, minutes later (Olivia has drifted away mentally but not physically) he comes back up the stairs with a small bag of jelly babies, procured from a corner shop still open, and sits down beside her to share them. And so the next phase of her life begins.

# 10

The young lawyer is Jonathan Altman. After the shared jelly babies, he disappears into the night, but he's taken her telephone number, and a day or two later, he rings.

'Olivia? This is Jonathan. A friend is having a party on Saturday – I wondered if you'd like to go?'

Jonathan's friends are sophisticated, political. At first, she feels a bit out of her depth, but quickly discovers that two or three of the guests have campaigned or protested with her own parents, and after a couple of glasses of wine she finds herself telling a story about the well-known activist who was a frequent visitor until the night he got so drunk that he fell asleep in the Martins' bath. There is laughter and encouragement to tell more, but she's careful not to overdo it. Jonathan watches her performance with indulgence and approval; by the time they leave the party she feels that she has passed a test.

Jonathan owns a city flat. When Olivia asks if his parents still live in the house Celeste once pointed out to her, he says no, his mother and father moved north some years ago; and while his flat is practical and convenient, he likes to spend the weekends out at Muizenburg, in a Victorian cottage he inherited from an aunt. The first time he takes Olivia there, she's deeply impressed by the immaculate, polished little house – the furniture is antique, the kitchen well-stocked, and the bed is a brass four-poster.

Bit by bit, she begins another personal transformation to meet Jonathan's requirements: the kohl-eyed, demi-monde look morphs into a more elegant image. She coils her hair at the nape of her neck and starts wearing the expensive hand-me-downs she's occasionally sent from Johannesburg by her father's sister. (Aunt Ianthe favours Olivia because she has never liked her brother's wife and takes a certain amount of pleasure in the fact that Olivia has caused her mother so much trouble.)

Slowly too, she starts to meet Jonathan's other friends, to go with him to plays and concerts, and to spend more and more of her nights in his flat – a top-floor apartment in a building overlooking the city's botanical gardens – or in the antique brass bedstead in Muizenburg. She's pretty sure Jonathan is in love with her, but she also knows he's tormented by her unsuitability as a potential wife. The problem is threefold: the men in her past (she makes no secret of them – what would be the point?) her lack of qualifications for a suitable career, and most of all, the fact that she isn't Jewish.

He talks a lot about his parents: his mother, whom he adores; his father, who's recovering from some life-threatening disease. Somewhere up north, they live their unknown lives in another gracious, antique-filled house – a place he describes to her as being always full of flowers, and where his mother gets up at dawn each day to cook, polish, supervise, cherish ... His father is also a lawyer, but because of his illness, about to retire; Jonathan is their blue-eyed boy, the apple of their collective eye, the son on whom all their hopes are pinned – which means that he's expected to marry a nicely brought-up, cultured, Jewish girl. Still, she loves him in a way that she hasn't loved anyone before, and in an effort to make up for her shortcomings, plays house with zeal whenever she can: she learns to cook the sort of food he likes, to arrange flowers and fruit, and to light the candles on Friday nights. She even goes with him one day to synagogue.

'Come with me to shul,' he said. 'I'd like you to.'

'Really?' Olivia is flattered, but nervous: she feels this is a test. 'Will I be able to sit with you?'

'No, I've told you, the women sit upstairs. But just do what everyone else does – you'll be fine.'

So she climbs the stairs and finds herself in a gallery full of women. It seems to her that they all turn to look at her, and that they know at once she isn't Jewish, but she murmurs 'Good Shavas' (as he's taught her) and tries to find an inconspicuous seat. It surprises her that the women seem so separate from what is taking place in the body of the building: the ritual chanting and singing are beautiful and compelling, but they don't always appear to pay much attention to it, talking softly amongst themselves and occasionally directing curious, but not unfriendly, glances in her direction. Their clothes look expensively fashionable – she feels under-dressed, an interloper, and she's relieved when the service is over.

Outside, as she waits for him under a flowering tree, she hears a voice at her shoulder.

'Olivia? I hardly recognised you! How are you?'

'Anton!' She hasn't seen him for several months – she throws her arms around him, kisses him. 'You've grown a beard!'

'And you – another transformation: you look wonderful! Are you off somewhere? Are you waiting for someone?'

She laughs, gesturing towards the synagogue. 'I've been to synagogue! With my boyfriend – here he comes now: Jonathan, this is Anton, an old friend of mine.'

But they know each other already.

Of course Anton knew Jonathan Altman – already he was being talked of as a man of conscience, a future leader – and Anton, now editing a student paper, and taking a growing interest in politics, had met him more than once. What has disconcerted him is seeing Altman with Olivia: Anton (in spite of his feelings for her – or possibly because of them) can't feel she is a suitably serious woman for Altman, a man he greatly admires. So, in a curious way, he finds himself doubly jealous: of Altman for having won Olivia, and of Olivia for having ensnared Altman.

'Well,' he shifts his feet uncomfortably, 'it was nice to run into you again ...' Or words to that effect. But Altman, with his easy charm, invites him down to Muizenburg, to the cottage.

'Come and have dinner some time. I'd like to talk to you about that article you wrote about the ANC.'

'It's my birthday next weekend,' Olivia chimes in. 'We've got some friends coming round on Saturday. Why don't you come too? Then you and Jonathan can have your intense political discussion while the rest of us more light-weight types slide gracefully under the table?' And she laughs up at him as she links her arm through Altman's.

He went, of course. He remembers the cottage very well – the evidence of money and taste, the polished furniture, the books – the dozen or so people that he met there, and the arrival of Joseph Kani just before he left. The only problem was that Altman himself wasn't there.

'So how do you know Anton de Waal?' Jonathan had asked her.

'He used to live close by. We were at primary school together.'

'Has he always been in love with you?'

'Anton? In love with me?' Olivia is taken aback. 'What makes you think that?'

'The way he looked at you. Are you sure there was never anything between you? No holding hands in the playground, or kisses behind the bike sheds?' Jonathan laughs. He's driving them back to his flat, but he takes one hand off the steering wheel to pat her knee. 'I wouldn't blame you, a nice-looking boy like that!'

Olivia is silent.

This is the problem: there are too many men in her past, and whenever they run into one of her old friends, Jonathan becomes uneasy. They've talked about this; they've agreed that it's grossly unfair that men should be able to sleep around with impunity while women are censured, but the fact remains: Olivia has a reputation that will dog her heels no matter how spotlessly faithful she is, no matter how devoted she proves herself to be. And Jonathan, she's beginning to suspect, will never be able to rid himself of suspicion and resentment.

Inside the flat, things get worse. There's a letter waiting, from his mother. She's coming down to Cape Town for one night only; she'll be staying with Jonathan, naturally, and she expects him to fetch her from the station. She plans to take him out to dinner and the theatre – a little treat, just for the two of them – and she'll go back home the following day. Unfortunately, the night in question is also the night of Olivia's birthday.

'I'm so sorry,' he says, 'but there's really nothing I can do about it. Maybe we could have your party on the Sunday instead?'

Olivia shakes her head. 'You know my parents are expecting us on Sunday,' she says. 'My mother's gone to a lot of trouble, and Cynthia and Simon are coming. I can't ask them to change their plans – it's too short notice.'

Of course, what she wants him to say is that her birthday party is more important – or even better, that he'll take her with him to meet his mother. In which case she'd cancel her party without a second thought. After all, she's already taken him home to meet her family: they were clearly impressed that she'd met such a serious, principled young man, and the evening had gone some way to repairing her relationship with them. It had also given her hope that Jonathan, in turn, would arrange a meeting with his parents.

Instead, he says, 'Well, why don't you go ahead and have your friends round anyway, and I'll take you somewhere nice the weekend after to make up?' and she has to turn away to hide her tears.

# 11

A week later, Jonathan drives them down to the cottage. The following day he'll go up to town to fetch his mother, leaving Olivia to finish making the preparations for her party on her own, but on this evening before her birthday, he gives her flowers, opens wine, cooks for her, and treats her with more than usual tenderness. Afterwards, in the big brass bed, his passion for her is both consuming and prolonged. He strokes her, rocks her in his arms, and whispers words of love with more intensity than usual. Then he falls asleep, quickly and easily, but Olivia lies awake with a cold sick knot in her stomach.

Tomorrow will be her twentieth birthday. It's the first time she's invited friends of her own to the cottage. She knows they're curious about her new lover (she's been looking forward to showing him off, to basking before them in her happiness) – and it's not just her friends: there are other couples, friends of Jonathan's, who will see this party as a validation of her place in his life. Except that now they won't. They'll see her instead for what she is, the girl he can't take to meet his mother, the mistress placated with wine and flowers. Tears of self-pity seep down her face, but in the end she sleeps, and by the time the first guests arrive on Saturday evening, she has her story ready.

'Poor Jonathan,' she says, 'he was distraught! But I told him, no, you have to go, she's your mother, and she's had a hard time with your father not being well – anyway, it's too soon to meet me. I mean, for that generation, the whole not-Jewish thing – never mind my job – the shock might kill her!' She pulls a comic face and flutters round them, pouring wine and beer, offering food. Her friends are impressed, she can see, with her surroundings, but it's Anton, surprisingly, who saves the day, because he arrives with a companion.

'Olivia,' he says, 'look who I bumped into today! Do you remember Patrick?'

And Olivia, who hasn't seen Patrick since the day of the ill-fated kite on Muizenburg beach all those years ago, recognises him instantly. He's even better-looking than she remembers, charming everyone, blinding them with his London glamour, seducing them with his stories. The tale of the kite becomes an uproarious saga; he tosses back the wine, blue eyes glinting, black hair falling to his shoulders, long legs in expensive boots hooked around the legs of his chair. They are all eating out of his hands, even the serious political ones, because Patrick, with the lightest of touches, establishes his credentials. The aged aunt he's staying with is a stalwart of the Black Sash, the women's organisation that Olivia's mother belongs to, that so bravely protests against the political situation – he thinks she might once have had a 'thing' with a well-known prisoner on Robben Island – and he mentions a brush with the Special

Branch on a recent visit to the home of a dissident writer. There's even a glancing reference to an aristocratic cousin with IRA connections.

Olivia has no idea how much of all this is true, but she doesn't care. The food has mostly been eaten but there's enough wine and beer left, and one of the boys has taken on the job of supervising the record-player. She's kicked off her shoes and is dancing with Anton and her friend Suzette. Her long skirt swirls and her hair ripples down her back as she closes her eyes and sways to the music. Against all the odds, her party is a success.

Then, just before midnight, she hears another car turn into the drive and her heart lifts at the sudden thought that perhaps it might be Jonathan after all: she's given her guests the impression that he's planning to return as soon as he can decently leave his mother. But it isn't Jonathan who knocks heavily on the door, it's the police.

To be precise, it is one policeman who stands on the doorstep. He is middle-aged, solid and polite.

'I'm sorry to disturb you, lady,' he says, 'but we've had a report about a suspicious individual in this area and we're checking all the properties in the neighbourhood.' While he speaks, his eyes are raking the room behind her; she can see a younger colleague in the passenger seat of the police van, talking into a hand-held receiver.

Luckily, someone had seen the van as it drew up and shouted a warning through into the kitchen: she'd told her friends that anyone wanting to smoke a joint could use the little back yard. Such small amounts of cannabis that remain will have been hurled over the wall into the bush, and the kitchen door is shut.

'No suspicious individuals here,' she says, smiling up at him, 'apart from my friends. It's my birthday.'

He gives a small smile in return. 'Well, many happy returns, 'Juffrou, but make sure when your friends leave that your doors and windows are securely bolted. And if you see anyone or anything suspicious, you must call the local station.' He gives her the number on a scrap of paper. 'Any outbuildings?' he asks, as an afterthought.

'No.' Olivia shakes her head and has a moment of panic in case he decides to walk around the back to check for himself: there could well be an incriminating smell. But Sergeant Van Wyk (he has a plastic name badge on his chest) is tired, and like so many men he has responded to Olivia's charm. Besides, he has children of his own: this lot might be lefty students but otherwise they look fairly harmless, so he says good night, and the van disappears back down the drive.

After that, the party begins to break up. Olivia does her best to keep it going – the truth is she's dreading the moment she'll be alone in this isolated little cottage – but there's a slight feeling of unease now, a general desire to get home to bed. 'Sorry we can't wait for Jonathan,' they say. 'Thanks for a fabulous party.'

Anton and Patrick are the last to go, but they're concerned about leaving her alone, perhaps they should wait for Jonathan to get back? She's saved from replying by another knock at the door.

This time she recognises the bulky young man on the doorstep. He's a law student, a friend of Jonathan's, she searches for his name – Richard? Raymond? Behind him is a thinner, darker shape.

'Olivia?' he says. 'It's Robert. Can we come in?' His voice is urgent.

Olivia holds the door wide. 'I'm afraid the party's over,' she says. 'The last two guests are just leaving!'

A look of alarm crosses Robert's face but vanishes when he sees Anton. Introductions are made: the thin dark boy in a threadbare jacket is called Joseph Kani, and he, too, is known to Anton.

'Where's Jonathan?' Robert is bundled up against the night chill, but his face has an unhealthy pallor and is glossed with sweat.

'Not back yet,' Olivia replies. 'He went up to town to see his mother. Why? What's the matter?'

Robert looks doubtfully at Patrick, but Anton gives a little nod. It's safe to talk.

'Joseph needs somewhere to stay tonight. I was taking him to a safe house, the other side of Muizenburg, but I saw police vans outside, so I had to drive on. He was on the floor, under a blanket.'

Olivia looks at Joseph. She knows she's seen him somewhere before. His face is expressionless, but he's shivering.

'I didn't know where else to go,' Robert continues, 'so I took a chance on Jonathan being here. When are you expecting him back?'

'I'm not sure,' says Olivia. 'It looks as though he's been held up.' She makes a quick decision: 'You can stay here, if you like. The police have been round already – they were looking for a 'suspicious individual'. I don't think they'll come back.'

'I tell you what,' says Anton, 'why don't I go ahead and drop Patrick off, then drive back home, and if I see any police activity, I can phone and tell you. In the meantime, you should probably turn off the lights to make it look as though you've gone to bed, then just sit tight and wait for Jonathan. If you agree, Olivia?'

Olivia agrees. She is afraid, as they all are – with good reason – of the security police, but she's still riding the tide of her party, and buoyed up by an unusual sense of her own importance: Jonathan, who should be taking charge, is absent, dancing attendance on his mother, while she – frivolous, lightweight Olivia – is proving to be the heroine of the hour.

'Are you quite sure, Olivia?' Anton asks again, and Patrick says, 'Good girl,' and winks before he kisses her goodbye. The wink tells her that he knows they're both taking a certain relish in the cloak and dagger nature of the drama. He recognises a fellow performer.

When the door closes behind them, Olivia switches out the lights, but leaves a lamp on in the bedroom and the door ajar to give a little light. The fire has died so she finds a blanket for Joseph Kani, who wraps himself in it gratefully. Then she makes hot, sweet tea for all three of them.

'I know you, don't I?' She says, handing Joseph his mug.

'We met a few years ago,' he replies, 'in your parents' house. You were going to your Matric dance.'

'Of course!' Olivia remembers the faint scar on his cheek. 'You were with your friend, the boy who was going overseas. What was his name?'

'Thabo.'

'Thabo, of course. How's he doing?'

'I think he is all right.'

Robert interrupts. 'Look here, Olivia, I feel bad about keeping you up like this. Do you have any idea when Jonathan will be back?'

He peers worriedly at his watch. 'It's past one – I need to get home soon myself. My wife hasn't been too well, and she'll be worried.'

Olivia hadn't known he was married: he looks too young, too overweight, untidy. He doesn't look as though anyone is taking care of him – but perhaps he hasn't got that sort of wife.

She makes another decision. 'I'm sure he won't be much longer, but why don't you go on home? It's not fair to worry your wife, especially if she's not well. Joseph can sleep on the sofa – he'll be safe here until tomorrow. But what about tomorrow?' She's suddenly remembered that Jonathan probably won't be back before midday.

It's Joseph who answers. 'Once it's daylight, no-one will notice me. There will be others around; I know where to go to meet the people who are helping me.'

She doesn't ask where he's going next, or why he's on the run, but he's probably heading north. He'll go across the border, to Mozambique perhaps.

Robert seems uncertain. Even a man of liberal convictions must feel a qualm at the thought of leaving a young white woman alone with a black man. On the other hand, Joseph seems like a decent man, and the woman in question is Olivia Martin: a free-spirited unconventional girl, if what he's heard is true. Anyway, Jonathan's bound to turn up soon, and he needs to get back to his wife. (Also, it will be a relief to get safely home himself. He'd undertaken to drop Joseph off, no more than that, and he's done the best he can.)

Robert shakes Joseph's hand, claps him on the back and wishes him well. Then, as she sees him out, he turns to Olivia and says impulsively, 'You're an amazing woman – I hadn't realised. Jonathan's a lucky man.'

*

Back inside, Olivia makes more tea. She also fetches a quilt from the bedroom, for herself. The room is becoming bitterly cold.

'Olivia,' Joseph says, 'I am very sorry. This isn't fair on you. I think I should go.'

'Don't be silly,' Olivia says. 'It's freezing out there, and it's raining. You'd catch your death even if you weren't picked up by the police. I'm just sorry I can't light the fire again, but I think Anton was right, it's better if it looks as though everyone's gone to sleep.'

'Well then, you should go to bed yourself. I can sleep on the sofa until Jonathan gets here.'

'All right,' she says, 'I'll just finish my tea.'

But she doesn't go to bed; instead, they start to talk. She asks him about himself, and he tells her – not about his journalistic activities or the grim reality of his daily life, but about his childhood in rural Natal; about herding goats and walking miles to school in his bare feet, about sleeping on the floor of his mother's hut, kept warm by siblings on either side. And she responds by telling him about her own childhood, about the time they went to look at the rock paintings, and the boy who took her hand to help her down from the caves.

'That could have been me,' Joseph says, and they both laugh.

They talk about their friends, their families; they find they share a love of books, and a yearning for other, safer times. In Joseph's voice she hears a terrible longing for his home. They don't talk about politics at all, or what is going to happen to either of them next.

Then, without warning, he gives a long, shuddering sigh and closes his eyes. Olivia can just make out the sheen of tears running down his cheeks.

'Oh Joseph,' she whispers, going over to crouch beside him, 'what is it?'

'It is your kindness,' he says simply.

'Oh, Joseph,' she says again, and as she feels his thin body begin to shake with sobs, she reaches out and takes him in her arms.

When Olivia wakes, Joseph is gone. There's no trace of his being there, which is a good thing because Jonathan's part-time maid (an unreliable woman called Frieda) has chosen this morning to come in and is muttering darkly to herself as she clears away debris from the night before.

Olivia and Frieda are not friends. Frieda doesn't think much of Olivia but she can't be sure she won't become a permanent fixture in her employer's life, so she treats her circumspectly; Olivia is uncomfortable with Frieda because she suspects the older woman despises her, so she apologises profusely for the mess and gets under Frieda's feet by trying to help, until it's made clear that her presence isn't wanted.

Sitting with a cup of coffee in a patch of winter sunshine in the garden, Olivia considers the events of the night before, and hopes that no-one saw Joseph leaving the cottage. Not that it matters from her point of view – she'll tell Jonathan all about it when he gets back – but she's desperate to know that he is safe. And for the first time in years, she sends up a prayer to the god she doesn't believe in, to deliver Joseph Kani from the evil that so clearly lies in wait.

# 12

The name of Joseph Kani rings on down the years: it crops up in many contexts and countries – even, decades later, in Italy, in Ascoli Piceno, where the sun is shining and Patrick, Anton and Marie-Claude are breakfasting on the terrace. This is a long-established custom: the view from the terrace is spectacular, and the somnolent rural peace a soothing contrast to their normal busy lives.

It's Patrick who suddenly stabs the newspaper he's reading and says, 'There's an interesting article here about Jonathan Altman.'

Anton looks up. 'He's been in the news a lot lately. What does it say?'

'That he's in line for the Joseph Kani Prize. All that work he did during the miners' stand-off a couple of years back, on top of a life-time's commitment to peace and reconciliation in South Africa. Weren't you thinking of writing a book on him yourself?'

Anton shrugs. 'I usually prefer my subjects to have been dead a bit longer, but yes, it's crossed my mind.'

'Well, now's the time,' says Patrick. 'Then someone can turn it into a film, and I can play him: one last great role before I retire.' He laughs; he hasn't the slightest intention of retiring, and even his enemies have to admit that he's aged extremely well, his dark, louche, elegance undeservedly transformed into silver, elder-statesman dignity. And he's earned more than enough money to pick and choose the roles he wants.

Marie-Claude also looks up from her magazine. 'You both knew Altman quite well, didn't you?'

'Not *that* well,' says Patrick. 'Anton had more to do with him than I did. It's ironic though that he's up for the Kani Prize, given the personal connection.'

'What personal connection, Patrick?' Marie-Claude waits expectantly – she has long experience of her cousin's habit of tossing conversational pebbles into tranquil pools.

'Joseph Kani was given shelter when he was on the run by Jonathan Altman's then-girlfriend – our mutual friend, Olivia Martin. Olivia, being the proverbial tart with a heart, gave him rather more comfort than was wise, and ended up having an abortion, or so the story goes. The Immorality Act at the time meant sex across the colour bar was illegal, so when she found out she was pregnant, she couldn't take the risk that Kani was the father. Abortion was also illegal, it goes without saying, so it was all hushed up, but the story got out anyway. Altman, being the honourable chap he was, arranged and paid for it all – at considerable risk to himself. Later, of course, Olivia achieved a sort of post-dated sainthood, as the woman who comforted Kani in his hour of need. I'm surprised you didn't know all this.'

'I don't think either of us has ever heard her talk about it,' says Anton shortly. 'Anyway, it's all water under the bridge now. Speaking of which, I think I might be ready for a swim ...' and he gets up and strolls across to the edge of the pool to test the temperature with his toe.

*

Olivia has no children. It isn't something she ever talks about, but Anton has from time to time wondered if it's been from choice, or because of the train of events that was set in motion after her twentieth birthday.

Some weeks after that memorable party, he'd run into her in Cape Town and congratulated her on her unexpected status as a heroine of the struggle.

'What on earth do you mean?' She looked at him blankly.

'The story has got out that you took in Joseph Kani and hid him all night even though you were on your own.'

'How do you know I was on my own, that Jonathan didn't come back?'

'Because he told Robert that by the time he got home the next day, Kani had gone.'

'Oh God. That explains it: I wondered why I was getting approving looks from some quarters.'

'Are you ok?' Anton asked. 'You look a bit tired.'

'It's being a heroine that's so exhausting! No, seriously, I'm not feeling great: some stomach bug I seem to have picked up. Dysentery, I shouldn't wonder.' She laughed. 'I probably shouldn't have kissed you!'

But of course, it was much simpler and more prosaic than that: Olivia, having been careless about taking her pill, was in the very early stages of pregnancy, and once this had been confirmed, events moved rapidly.

The Altmans have an old family friend, a doctor, whom Jonathan goes to see. As abortion is illegal in South Africa, the friend would not normally be party to any such activity, but Jonathan is the son of his oldest friend, and when the tragic facts of the case are made known to him – that a misguided young woman has been taken advantage of by a black man, but that Jonathan is standing by her in order to preserve her reputation – he reluctantly agrees to help.

So, this is what happens: early one evening, a man carrying a doctor's bag arrives at the flat. He's clearly unhappy about the work he has agreed to do and understandably wants to get it over with as quickly as possible. He asks Jonathan to leave the room, and does what he's come to do brusquely, efficiently, and in silence. She lies with her knees spread and cries, also in silence.

It doesn't take long. He's injected some sort of caustic substance into her womb, which will eventually induce bleeding. For perhaps five or ten minutes after he leaves, she's alone. Is Jonathan being given advice and instructions on what to do next? Seeing the doctor down to his car? Handing over a discreet envelope? She doesn't know or care – she's simply overwhelmed by grief, humiliation, loneliness and pain.

There's a window beside the bed from where she can see down to the busy evening street, several storeys below. The thought of oblivion is briefly appealing, but she's already destroying one life, and anyway, she might land on some innocent passer-by rather than hit a vacant stretch of pavement. So she closes her eyes and waits for Jonathan to return and the bleeding to begin. When this happens, she can be admitted to a private clinic where her womb will be scraped out, a lot of money will change hands, and no questions will be asked.

When Jonathan comes back into the room, Olivia is lying with her face pressed into the pillow, weeping. He's distraught, solicitous; he even cries as he strokes her brow and tells her she hasn't deserved this. And when eventually she starts to bleed, he helps her gently downstairs and drives her to the clinic, where no-one expresses either curiosity or sympathy as she is booked in, led away, undressed, sedated, and wheeled to theatre on a trolley. They all know very well why she's there. When she wakes up, she's back in the recovery room and she is no longer pregnant.

Olivia moves through the next few weeks like a sleepwalker, or an invalid recovering from an illness. The story she puts about is that she's had a relapse of a virus she had as a child – if her friends and family have any other suspicions, they don't voice them – and she confides only in Celeste and Suzette that she and Jonathan are having some time apart.

But even before this, the name of Joseph Kani is being splashed across the papers: he has been apprehended outside Johannesburg and taken for interrogation at John Vorster Square, the prison where he subsequently dies. He's said to have hanged himself in his cell, but by this stage so many prisoners have died in this prison that the general belief, amongst those who care, is that he succumbed to torture. Olivia hears the news at a party.

It's Suzette who persuades her to go. 'Come on,' she says. 'I know you've been sick, and things are rocky with Jonathan, but he was out last week with Rachel Wolf – I'm sorry but Alida told me, and you need to know – so you've got to get out there sooner or later and show your face. Anyway, it'll do you good to see some of your friends again.'

It's true, she's been out of circulation since her birthday, and she feels guilty for neglecting Suzette, who's a good friend. She also feels bad that she hasn't told her the truth about what happened, but in fact she's told no-one, because she's so deeply ashamed. She's twenty years old and has no qualifications or means of support other than her poorly-paid modelling, and she knows very well that she couldn't have kept the baby. All the same, she feels a burden of guilt that she didn't somehow manage to stand up against the rest of them, for herself, for her child, for her outraged sense of justice. But there's no point in dwelling on any of this, so she makes up her face, dresses flamboyantly, and accompanies Suzette to the party.

The house is in Mowbray, a pleasant, shabby, rambling family home belonging to a young lecturer at the university and his wife, who is a potter. They have a baby of their own which is being passed around while Marie fetches plates of food from the kitchen and Francois pours drinks for the collection of academics, journalists and students who make up the bulk of the guests.

The first inkling Olivia gets that she's become the subject of further gossip is when a girl called Ruth corners her and takes both her hands in a painful grip.

'Olivia,' she says, 'I just wanted to say that I am *so* sorry: my heart goes out to you for what you've been through.'

This is a bit more than any normal commiseration on a break-up with Jonathan – particularly as Ruth is an admirer of his, and up until now has shown no sign that she admires Olivia – and she doesn't think she can be referring to her small part in helping Joseph Kani. Several other exchanges now begin to strike her as odd, but it's only when someone holds the baby out to her and Marie hastily intervenes and says, 'Don't bother Olivia with him, I need her to tell me what she thinks of my new pots,' that she begins to suspect that somehow the story of her abortion has got out. Final confirmation comes from Suzette, who, flushed with drink and torn between sympathy and hurt, whispers, 'Why didn't you *tell* me you were pregnant?'

Olivia has had several glasses of wine herself. She's accepted plates of food from various solicitous men, and now catches the eye of Dracula, who has brought Mrs Dracula to the party and who motions her over to join them at a long table pushed against the wall.

Mrs Dracula has russet hair and sleepy eyes, and she either doesn't know or doesn't care what her husband gets up to with his models. She pats Olivia's hand, admires her dress, and is just beginning to tell her about a woman in Woodstock who makes wonderful clothes, when a boy Olivia knows, but whose name she has forgotten, bursts into the room and asks if they've heard the news? Joseph Kani is dead.

There's a dreadful silence, during which the boy catches sight of Olivia and everyone else tries not to look at her. Olivia herself puts her head down on the table and begins to sob – for herself, for her lost child, and for the young man she barely knew.

The only other thing that happens is that Jonathan comes to see her and offers her a plane ticket to London. This is a neat solution to several problems: it will take Olivia away for a while and give her a chance to make a fresh start; it will assuage his own feelings of guilt and give him a breathing space in which to assess his future; and it seems to him a generous enough present to make up to Olivia for what she's gone through in the last few months – after all, air travel from South Africa is still beyond the reach of most people: the usual route for the young is by Union Castle liner, in the cheapest possible cabin.

Anton sees her one more time before she leaves the country. His own military service is looming, so they're both facing an uncertain future when they meet in a café in Long Street. He's there first, but he knows the moment she walks in, because there's a break in the buzz of conversation, and as she comes towards him, he sees that yet another transformation has taken place.

Her face is thinner, and the sophisticated elegance of her Jonathan period has been replaced by a dramatic gypsy look: her hair is wild and loose, silver hoops swing from her ears. She looks defiant, and somehow younger.

'Another new Olivia!' he says. 'You look wonderful.'

She kisses him. 'I'm trying to live up to my reputation as both a dangerous, loose woman, and a heroine of the struggle.'

For a moment Anton doesn't know what to say. The problem is that he's loved Olivia for so long – and he admires her for having had the courage to shelter Joseph Kani – but at the same time he can't understand how she could have caused such pain to Jonathan Altman, a man for whom he has the deepest respect. In the end he simply takes both her hands in his and says, 'I'm so sorry, Olivia – for everything you've been through.'

She squeezes his hands and blinks to hide her tears. 'Oh well, at least I'm still alive. But I don't want to talk about all that. I want to know how *you* are, Anton. Are you dreading army life? When do you have to go?'

'Yes, and next week. But I've got into the Navy, which isn't so bad, and it's only a year: I'll get through it – most people do. And when it's done, I'm going to find some way of getting to England too. When do you leave yourself?'

'In a couple of weeks. I'm staying for Cynthia's wedding, then I'm off.'

'Have you got somewhere to stay?'

'Yes, there's an old cousin of my mother's, who lives in Wiltshire, I'll be staying with her at first. I can't work officially, of course, but I'm told it's quite easy to get a job as an au pair. South African girls are considered a cut above the usual run of foreigners, or so I've heard – white ones at any rate! – because they speak English. And then I'll see if I can find a way to extend my visa.'

'You don't think you'll come back?'

'Not if I can help it,' says Olivia.

What Anton didn't know, because she didn't tell him, or anyone else for that matter, was the truth: that Joseph Kani – hunted, captured, tortured and now dead – was not the cause of her break-up with Jonathan. In the emotional turmoil of the weeks during which Olivia's pregnancy was at first suspected, then confirmed, the problem became clear: Jonathan would not marry her. His parents – who had made such sacrifices for him and were so proud of him and the work that he was doing – would never accept her, and it wouldn't be fair to either of them to jeopardise the future with what might well turn out to be a disastrous marriage. They were both so young, he said –

given time, things could be different. In the meantime, maybe an overseas trip would give her time to think about going back to university to acquire some qualifications? Or even do a course? Antique restoration, cookery – there were so many possibilities! He told her he still loved her – would always love her – that this was a terrible decision for them both, but that for the time being there was nothing else that they could do.

Olivia said very little. Shame and humiliation prevented her, and when Jonathan told her that he had persuaded a doctor to help them terminate her pregnancy, she asked for no details; she simply let it happen.

What she didn't know, at the time, was that Jonathan had recently met a girl called Rachel who was a much more serious prospect as a wife; and the story going the rounds about the foolish young woman who'd got herself into trouble as the result of a liaison with a black fugitive (but whose decent white boyfriend had been prepared to risk his own future in order to help her) wasn't one he was going to contradict. It was only much later that she understood the full extent of Jonathan's relief that she was so unprotected, so unlikely to cause trouble, and in the end, so easily dealt with.

So it was that, a week after Cynthia got married in a long white dress and clouds of orange blossom, Olivia climbed aboard a plane at D.F.Malan Airport, and on a clear blue day in December, just before Christmas, flew off into the future.

# 13

'I was in London at the start of the seventies, too,' says Liam, decades later. 'It was a bit of a shock to a boy from Enniskillen, I can tell you.'

'Maybe we passed each other in the street.'

'No,' says Liam. 'I would have stopped, for sure. I would have known you were the one for me, even in a London crowd.'

Olivia laughs, leaning forward to kiss him. 'What a pity we didn't meet, we might have saved each other a lot of trouble! What were you doing there, anyway?'

'I went over with a bunch of student friends. We got night shift work in a bakery and shared a terrible room in Earl's Court.'

'I was living in Camden,' says Olivia. 'Did you ever go to Camden Lock?'

The new market at Camden Lock hadn't been open long, but already it was the place to go to, and at weekends the craft workshops and kaleidoscopic variety of stalls drew Olivia like a magnet. Her weekdays and nights were mostly spent in the chaotic Camden house in which she'd found a job as an au pair. As with so many of her plans, what actually happened turned out to be slightly different from what she had envisaged: the liberal, cultivated London family of her imagination, whose children went to violin and ballet lessons, and whose kitchen had Elizabeth David casseroles bubbling on the Aga, had been replaced by the reality of Carolina and Marie-Ange Delgado.

Carolina is a Venezuelan divorcee, whose house is a kaleidoscopic jumble of valuable antiques and junk stall tat; where there is a Hockney in the sitting-room, and Art Nouveau mirrors look down on a shifting population of friends, relatives, fugitives, and artists of one sort or another, as well as whatever dogs, cats, parrots and other small animals are currently being given refuge. The moment Olivia steps over the threshold, she is in thrall.

Carolina herself is difficult, to say the least: a woman with no sense of time or order, whose moods and affections change from hour to hour. Luckily, Marie-Ange, her four-year-old daughter, is well-named: she has the placid, blonde serenity of a small angel, and takes to Olivia on sight. They walk to the park, to the shops, play games and read books together; then while Marie-Ange sleeps, Olivia attempts to do some basic housekeeping. This isn't easy, given the number of temporary residents, both human and animal, that Carolina collects, but she does her best. A proper au pair, of course, would have had mornings or afternoons free to go to language classes, but Carolina has seized on Olivia precisely because she has no need of lessons. She wants her to teach Marie-Ange as much English as possible, and she wants her there whenever she needs her. This means that the hours are erratic, but the pay is generous, and there's the added bonus of the often interesting and glamorous people who come and go – one of whom turns out to be an old acquaintance.

'Olivia,' says Carolina, coming into the kitchen with an armful of flowers and a bag full of bottles, 'I have some friends coming round this evening. What have we got to eat?'

'Not a lot,' says Olivia, opening the fridge. 'Left-over bolognaise, eggs, cheese ... There was a chicken, but I think Alfredo and his friend ate it.'

Carolina clicks her tongue – Alfredo is a distant cousin who drifts by from time to time, to see what he can find to eat. 'Never mind, we'll order pizza, that will do. Querida!' Belatedly, she embraces Marie-Ange, who is eating her supper at the kitchen table and waiting patiently to be noticed. 'Cómo estás, mi pequeña? Olivia is going to help Mummy with the flowers and then she can give you your bath. Olivia, see if you can find some empty vases, and a clean cloth ...' She drifts out again to answer the phone, which is shrilling in the hall.

When Marie-Ange has been bathed, read to, and tucked up in bed with the latest stray – a ginger kitten – curled up beside her, Olivia goes to her own room to exchange her jeans and T-shirt for a trailing, multi-coloured skirt and top. She attaches long dangling earrings to her ears and pins her hair up loosely with a couple of purloined flowers. (Carolina won't mind: another of her reasons for employing Olivia is that she likes to be surrounded by decorative people.) Then she goes downstairs to open the door to the pizza deliveryman. Except that it isn't the deliveryman on the doorstep, but Patrick Luke.

'I'm a little early, I'm afraid,' says Patrick – then stops dead. 'Olivia? Good God! Olivia – what on earth are you doing here?'

'I'm the au pair,' says Olivia. 'I've been here nearly three months.'

'Well, I'm blowed!' Patrick steps into the hall and sweeps her off her feet, whirling her round and laughing delightedly – to the bemusement of Carolina, who is descending the stairs in a cloud of Opium.

'Carolina, darling, how wonderful you look! And how extraordinary that Olivia is your au pair!'

As drinks are poured, Patrick explains how they know each other, and somehow manages to flatter them both at once by inferring that Olivia is lucky to be employed by someone like Carolina, and that Carolina is lucky to have Olivia as her au pair. Patrick's charm, she sees, is as potent as ever, and his personal attractions have been increased by the fact that he's about to start work with an award-winning British director on a film in which he has a major part. No-one – least of all Patrick – doubts for an instant that he'll be a star.

'And you, Olivia? Tell me what's been happening to you?'

'Well, I stayed in Winchester with a cousin when I arrived, but I really wanted to get to London, so I looked for a job as an au pair, and I found Carolina and Marie-Ange.'

Life with Cousin Sybil had been set in an unshakeable routine of dog-walking, bridge twice a week, church on Sunday, and evenings in front of the television. This last activity was briefly addictive – Olivia, like all South Africans of her generation, had been deprived of television – but it also showed her just what she was missing: the explosion of pop culture and youthful rebellion that seemed to be centred on London. By the middle of January, the novelty of snowy country walks and fireside teas had worn off completely, and she began to scour the advertisements for nannies and au pairs, which eventually resulted in a day of interviews in London, and her fateful meeting with Carolina. Olivia's tourist visa didn't allow her to work, of course, but the city was full of young foreigners being paid in cash and managing to stay below the official radar. So, to prove that she had sufficient funds to support herself, she borrowed from Cousin Sybil (who had done her duty nobly but was secretly relieved at the prospect of this particular cuckoo leaving her nest) and succeeded in extending her stay.

All this she tells Patrick later in the evening, when Carolina is sufficiently engrossed in her other guests (particularly a bearded American reputed to own a fabulous art collection) to allow them to defect to a nearby pub. There, she asks Patrick about his part in the film – 'I am the mysterious and fatally attractive young man who comes to stay, and seduces both his hostess and his host,' he says, leering horribly – and then she asks if he has any news of Anton.

'Poor love,' Patrick says, 'He's still doing his naval service. The last I heard he was stuck on some hideous ship out in the Atlantic. He's planning to move over here as soon as he's finished: it appears that his mother, although she's lived in South Africa since she was a baby, was actually born in the UK, so he can apply for citizenship. We'll be able to have a celebratory reunion – if *you're* still here, that is.'

Olivia pulls a face. 'My mother wasn't considerate enough to get born over here, so I've only got until the end of July. After that they'll probably throw me out.'

'Unless you can find someone to marry,' says Patrick. Then he waves at a group of people who've just come in through the door in a flurry of noise and laughter. 'Nick! Over here! Come and meet Olivia.'

Nick is a musician, the girl with him has long, red hair and an embroidered gypsy shawl; she's an actress, and her name, apparently, is Delilah. There's another, paler, quieter girl, and a couple of shaggy-haired boys, one of whom slips into the seat beside Olivia.

'Hello,' he says, 'I'm Michael.'

Whatever else Michael may be, Olivia can see straight away he isn't marriage material. For one thing, he's patently in love with Patrick. Slight, fair, grey-eyed, he watches him with the devotion of one worshipping at a shrine. Patrick, for his part, treats him with the offhand affection of an older brother. 'Be kind to Michael,' he leans across to tell Olivia. 'He's an innocent country boy who's not used to city girls.'

'I'm not used to them myself,' says Olivia, watching Delilah wind an arm around Patrick's neck to draw him back into her conversation. 'Where are you from, Michael?'

'Northern Ireland. From a small farm north of Belfast, which according to Patrick means I've still got mud on my boots and hayseed in my hair.'

He smiles at her, a wary, self-mocking smile, and Olivia finds herself warming to him. 'Well, I've never been to Belfast, but from what I've seen on the news, you're a lot safer in London – even if it is full of wicked city girls!' She laughs, then says more soberly, 'It must be horrible though, trying to live a normal life with all that going on. Has your family been affected by the troubles?'

'Oh, we're all affected, one way and another,' says Michael, 'but yes, I had a good friend who was killed last year, and one of my sisters is a nurse, she's seen some terrible things.'

'I'm sorry,' says Olivia, and reaches out to pat his hand. 'So, what are you doing in London?'

'Selling books,' he says, 'and trying to write one – besides getting away from bloody Belfast, of course. What about you?'

'Au-pairing, and getting away from bloody South Africa,' she replies, aware as she speaks that a bond is forming between them. This is hardly surprising: they're both outsiders, marked out by their accents and the fact that they come from places where violence and cultural lunacy seem to be the order of the day. Then she turns back to Patrick, in answer to something he has asked, and the conversation becomes general.

Michael watches them closely. Patrick, as always, is effortlessly the centre of attention: he's not famous yet, but people always stop and look at him again. Delilah is an attention-grabber too – confident, polished; they both take adulation as their due. Olivia, on the other hand, in spite of her flamboyant clothes and air of independence (and to Michael, the exotic charm of her accent and suntanned skin) has something vulnerable about her. So when she makes a move to leave – 'No Patrick, I must go. Someone needs to be there for Marie-Ange. Carolina could have forgotten all about her by now and gone off to a club' ('More likely in bed with the American,' says Patrick) – Michael writes his phone number on a piece of paper, gives it to her, and says 'Let's meet up for coffee.'

Olivia, delighted to have connected with Patrick again, and to have made a new friend in Michael, goes home feeling unusually happy. But just a few days later everything changes, when Carolina announces – out of the blue – that she must return to Venezuela, and Olivia discovers that she has exactly two weeks to find somewhere else to live. Cousin Sybil is unfortunately going away herself (or so she says) and Olivia, who has been living rent-free and spending most of her money on clothes and entertainment, is thrown into a panic. No-one else is going to want to take on an au pair for the short time remaining on her visa, and even the cheapest room in a shared flat will be beyond her means.

It's Michael who comes to the rescue. When they meet for coffee, she pours out her tale of woe: 'Total disaster,' she says, 'Carolina's going home at the end of the month, so it's either out on the street for me, or back to Cape Town before my visa is up, with my tail between my legs!'

'You could sleep on our sofa,' Michael offers. 'It's not very comfortable, I'm afraid, but one of Kevin's friends used it for a few weeks at Christmas, and I don't think the others would mind. I'll check with them tonight and let you know.'

Michael shares a flat in Kentish Town with Lucy and Claire, who are sisters, and Kevin, an Australian barman. They are all quite willing for Olivia to move in and sleep on the sofa, in return for doing her share of the domestic chores. Accordingly, she spends the next two weeks frantically rehousing as many of Carolina's pets as she can – the ginger kitten moves next door, two older cats already spend long periods away, so she assumes that they have other lives and leaves them to their fate, and the dogs she arranges to send to a shelter. The parrot also finds a home with a neighbour, and the rabbits are removed by Cousin Alfredo, possibly to eat, although she hopes not. Carolina herself is far too absorbed in her own plans to give much thought to the animals, but she's grateful to Olivia for making all the arrangements and rewards her with a considerable wad of cash when they finally say goodbye. Marie-Ange hugs and kisses her affectionately, but otherwise behaves with the stoicism she has needed to cultivate in order to survive life with her mother.

Olivia moves into the Kentish Town flat, and another chapter begins. She gets on well with Lucy and Claire – nice middle-class girls from Kent, playing at being bohemians while they complete their university studies. They are out a lot of the time, and Kevin, because of his working hours, isn't around that much either; only Michael is at home most evenings. Olivia (who can't afford to go out) has taken over the bulk of the cooking, and the two of them often eat together. On his days off, he sometimes joins her on cheap visits to galleries and museums, and on one occasion they share a tent in a damp field outside Bath, when they travel down with friends in a rattletrap van to a weekend pop concert. Bit by bit, they get to know each other.

One evening Michael comes home early, surprising Olivia who is sitting at the kitchen table, working on a drawing. She's begun to sketch again recently, spending some part of each day out in the nearby streets and squares and parks.

'That's really good,' he says, leaning over her shoulder. Then he leafs through her sketchbook while she checks to see if the stew is ready.

'I'm a bit rusty. It's been a while since I've done any drawing.'

'You should do something with them – sell them in the market or make them into cards.'

Olivia shrugs. 'There's not much point. I've got to leave the country when my visa's up.'

'Well,' says Michael, 'I've been thinking about that, and I want to talk to you about an idea I've had. It could be a solution to both our problems ...'

# 14

The day after Anton and Marie-Claude get back from their holiday in Ascoli Piceno, Marie-Claude picks up the phone, and Anton hears her say 'Yassine? How are you?' Then she switches to French, and her voice fades as she moves away.

Anton feels mildly put-out. He's the one who brought Yassine to Marie-Claude's attention in the first place, after all, when the boy sent him an invitation to an exhibition of student work. Marie-Claude had another engagement that evening, and it was only because it was cancelled at the last minute that she'd opted to come along.

The exhibition had been the usual mixture of the promising, the pretentious and the pedestrian. Yassine's work though, was patently in a class of its own, a series of portraits that commanded instant attention. There were eight all told, seven of unknown Londoners – Turkish, Chinese, African, an elderly white woman in a yellow coat, their features melting into strange, dream-like backgrounds – but the last face was instantly recognisable as that of Marie-Claude's cousin, the well-known actor, Patrick Luke.

Yassine had painted it – not from life, of course, but from a photograph – and it was Marie-Claude's decision to buy the portrait as a birthday present for her cousin that set future events in train. For Yassine, it was a stroke of good fortune that led inevitably to others: Marie-Claude took him up and arranged for him to meet Patrick, who (instantly besotted) commissioned, in turn, a portrait of Marie-Claude. There was an article in The Guardian, talk of a show in New York...all of which just went to show how unexpectedly things could turn out. Or not. Anton isn't entirely convinced that Yassine, having taken his card, hadn't checked out his details and somehow discovered his connection to Patrick Luke, and for that very reason chosen Patrick as a subject. The more he gets to know him, the more he realises that Yassine leaves nothing to chance. Not that he begrudges him his good fortune, but all the same, his nose is slightly out of joint. He feels excluded from the little triangle, and it's partly because of this that he decides to get in touch with Olivia and arrange to visit her. Which is why, a month or so later, soon after Marie-Claude and Patrick have departed, with Yassine, for a preliminary meeting with a gallery in New York, Anton himself takes a morning flight from Heathrow to Belfast.

*

As the plane begins to descend through the mist, he recognises the gash of Strangford Lough, and beyond that the waters of Belfast Lough. He remembers the three-month period that he worked in Belfast, back in the seventies, and the one and only time he took the ferry across to Liverpool. It had been a rough passage, the boat full of drunken soldiers (celebrating the end of a tour of duty) and a party of frightened school children on their way to France. Several of the passengers had been sick in their seats. He's had the odd rough plane journey too, but the descent today is reasonably smooth, and the woman in the seat next to him smiles with relief as they touch down.

'Not bad,' she says. 'Just as well – I wouldn't want to set anything off before time!' And she pats her visibly swollen stomach.

'When's your baby due?' asks Anton.

'Still three months to go,' she replies, 'but it's twins, that's why I'm so big.'

'I have twin sons,' says Anton. 'It was a lot of work at the start, but later on the benefits were considerable: there was always someone to play with.'

'Or fight with!' she responds. 'We've got two wee boys already' – she rolls her eyes comically – 'but you wouldn't be without them now, would you?'

'No, you wouldn't,' he agrees, and feels an unexpected wave of gratitude for his own wife and sons.

Olivia is there to pick him up at the airport. It's close to Belfast's new Titanic Quarter and has been renamed George Best City Airport since his last visit. (The people in this country seem to have a natural flair for turning disaster into profit – look at all those Troubles-related murals and former scenes of murder and destruction that are now visited by eager tourists.) Olivia herself is looking thinner, her dark hair more thickly striped with grey – like a badger emerging from a long winter.

'I picked up a cold on the flight back from Cape Town,' she says. 'I couldn't shake it off for weeks. The weather hasn't helped either.'

Banks of cloud are piling up above the choppy waters of the lough – the wind has a hard chill and the roads are wet with recent rain – but it's beautiful nonetheless; he remembers so well this shifting light on the green and purple of the hills, and the long, curving shore of the bay.

'Do you still go up the Cave Hill?'

'I do. It's one of Liam's favourite walks.'

Anton knows about Liam: he hasn't yet met him in the flesh, but Olivia talks about him easily. Inevitably, he's married, but the relationship has lasted several years and he has to admit she seems happy.

'Do you think there's any chance you'll ever live together?' he asks.

She shrugs. 'God knows. I'm so used to living on my own now, and his wife's an invalid you know. It would be very hard for him to leave her – but we manage. She goes to stay with his sister now and then. I've never liked the secrecy, of course, but I accepted long ago that it was the only way.'

'Is it just because of her illness that he's never left her, or does religion play a part? Or maybe the fact that he's very well-known?'

Olivia shrugs. 'All those things – you know what it's like here.'

He does indeed.

When, all those years ago in 1971, Anton finally arrived in London, his naval service done at last, Olivia had disappeared.

'Married, and gone to live in Northern Ireland,' said Patrick. 'Didn't I tell you?'

'No,' Anton replied. 'The last news I remember having from you was that she was working as an au pair.'

'Oh yes, that must have been just before we started filming. I think her visa was about to run out and she didn't want to go back home, so when I introduced her to Michael, it was the perfect solution for them.' Patrick paused, seeing Anton's blank expression, and explained: 'Michael comes from Ballybackward-in-the-Bog and needed to marry a woman to get his family off his back.'

'Are you telling me this Michael is gay?'

'Well, of course,' said Patrick. 'And unless he got married, he was going to be disinherited, crossed out of the family bible, responsible for sending his poor old mother into an early grave, etc, etc. So, they got married in a Registry Office and flew home to Belfast to present the family with a fait accompli. You're not upset, are you?' Patrick peered at him more closely. 'Anton! Don't tell me you're still carrying a torch for Olivia?'

'No, of course not. I'm just surprised, that's all.'

If Patrick knew he was lying, he gave no sign of it. Instead, he said 'I'll bet they were surprised in Ballybackward too! I'd have given a lot to have been there when Michael turned up with a heathen hussy in tow – and a foreigner to boot. They must have been reeling!'

'Oh, come on, that's not fair!'

'What's not fair? 'Heathen' or 'hussy'? I grant you she's white – and from their point of view, at least she's not a Catholic – but apart from that, she's hardly marriage material. They'll be preaching sermons about the Whore of Babylon in their midst, you mark my words!'

'What do you mean, *hardly marriage material?*' Anton sounded uncharacteristically angry, but Patrick shrugged.

'Apart from being foreign? No money, no proper qualifications or job, looks like a hippie, murky past ...'

'The last could be said of you too!'

'Well, of course,' said Patrick, 'but it's different for men, and you know it. Still, his parents will probably be so relieved he's got a woman – that he's *normal* after all – that they'll accept her. And you, my friend' – Patrick threw an arm around his shoulders – 'if you *were* still harbouring a slight tendresse for Olivia, then all I can say is, you've had a lucky escape. She's much too dangerous for you. I'll tell you who you ought to marry, though, now I come to think of it, and that's my cousin Marie-Claude. She's a cut or two above you, of course, but for some reason she always asks after you – and she's coming over to London next weekend.'

Anton and Marie-Claude *do* get married, in the end (with Patrick as Best Man stealing all the limelight) but long before then – after Marie-Claude has returned to France, and Patrick has flown off to Hollywood to start work on the film that will make him a household name, Anton is taken on as a trainee reporter by the BBC. Six months later, he finds himself on a three-month attachment to Belfast.

Belfast in 1972 is a place any sensible traveller avoids. The last four years have been a litany of horror; of riots and bombs and burned-out houses, of tanks and soldiers on the streets, and civilians blown to kingdom come as they stop for a pint, or board a bus, or simply walk down a road at the wrong time.

The pictures are seared on the world's eye: a priest waving a blood-soaked white handkerchief, a child's shoe lying beside a heap of smoking rubble, bits of bodies being shovelled into plastic bags. But the world moves swiftly on, and these pictures are soon replaced by others. The newsroom itself is a place of surprising energy and camaraderie: the community might be tearing itself apart, but the reporters are a team. Catholics and Protestants alike mock him for his foreign ignorance, but their non-partisan professionalism impresses him, as does their courage, and their humour. Despite the seemingly endless rain, the grim realities of the daily bombs and shootings, of dreary, time-consuming queues at checkpoints and barricades, Anton finds himself strangely happy. And, of course, he has reconnected with Olivia.

They live in a tiny, terraced house off the Ormeau Road. There's a narrow single bed in a cramped back bedroom, hardly bigger than a cupboard, where Anton sleeps the first time he visits.

'You can't possibly go home now,' Olivia says, when, shortly before midnight, he makes a move to leave. 'You won't be safe on the street at this time. Stay here.'

'Please,' says Michael. 'There's a spare bed – it's not up to much but it's better than being shot.'

So he sleeps, fitfully at first, disturbed by the wailing of sirens, the insistent rattle of helicopters overhead, the distant shots or explosions; but eventually exhaustion and the evening's wine and whiskey send him into a dreamless sleep. When he wakes it's after nine; a quiet Saturday morning, sunlight coming through the window. Olivia, downstairs, alone, is reading the morning paper.

'Tea?' She gestures at the pot. 'Michael's gone for his morning run, he'll stop by the bakery for something for breakfast on his way back, but there's cereal if you're starving.'

'Tea is fine.' He sits down opposite her at the table and notices the headline. 'Another bad night, I see.'

'Yes,' says Olivia. 'But at least it wasn't too bad around here. Did you manage to sleep?'

'Eventually. I hope it wasn't an imposition, having me here ...' he trails off, embarrassed. There are only two rooms at the top of the stairs, and through the open door he has seen that the other room contains a double bed.

'If you mean, were you taking up someone's bed, no. Michael and I share a bed. I suppose Patrick told you it was a marriage of convenience? Well, it's true, it was – but it's a lot more than that. We're not the usual sort of lovers, Anton, but we do love each other.'

It had surprised him, when he arrived the previous evening, to see the measure of affection between them, the obvious pleasure in each other's company.

'But ... is that going to be enough for you?' He can't help asking.

Olivia shrugs. 'Probably not. One of us is bound to fall in love with someone else at some point in the future, but we'll face that when we come to it. In the meantime, it's a very ...' she searches for the right words, 'a very healing partnership. For both of us.'

'I'm glad,' he says, and he is, although at the same time he feels deflated. 'It's funny, isn't it, when I knew I was coming over here, I thought I might persuade you to leave – I was planning on rescuing you! I mean, Belfast, of all the bloody cities in the world! But after three weeks I'm actually starting to like the place myself, and listening to you and Michael talk last night, I can see why you've stayed – in spite of all the shit that's going on.'

'It's something about the people,' Olivia says. 'As they say here, what you see is what you get – it might not be what you like, but at least you know where you are. They're really tough, but they're also kind, funny, down to earth ... and no-one's been anything other than welcoming to me.'

Anton has already discovered this for himself. In his opinion, this is a largely working-class war, and there are whole areas of the city where people seem barely affected. Their children go to school unmolested, they play golf and bridge, and it is only when they have to venture into the city centre, or travel further afield, that the reality bites home: the armoured cars, the young, nervous, soldiers holding rifles, the endless security checks and roadblocks. Across the border, on the other hand, life is still blessedly normal, and weekends in Donegal or Dublin are as prized as a trip to Paris would once have been. So, some weeks later, when Michael and Olivia are offered a few days in a friend's cottage in Donegal, and invite Anton to join them, he seizes the opportunity.

The car, borrowed from one of Michael's cousins, is old and slow: by the time they reach their destination on the north-west coast, it's already dark – the deep thick black of the countryside – and it's not until the morning, when he throws back the solid wooden shutters of his bedroom that he sees the bay. The cottage looks out over a patch of jade-green grass to a scatter of boulders, and then the sea; to the right, there's a ribbon of white beach, dunes and distant mountains; and directly opposite, in the middle of the bay, is a little island. There are sheep dotted everywhere, gulls crying overhead, and below him, shaking a cloth over the grass, is Olivia.

'Come down,' she calls. 'Breakfast's ready.'

There are duck eggs from a neighbour, and the rich moist wheaten bread that Anton has come to crave. And cup after cup of tea.

'Doesn't anybody else in this country drink coffee?' he asks. 'I'm not complaining about the tea – I like it – it's just I never seem to drink anything else.'

'What? Not even in the newsroom?' Olivia raises her eyebrows. 'I thought reporters lived on cigarettes and coffee.'

'Cigarettes and tea,' he says, 'or something stronger.'

'My mother has a jar of Nescafe for visitors,' says Michael, 'but the tea's the thing. Strong enough to trot a mouse on, as my father likes to say.'

'God, I thought the tea would kill me!' Olivia pulls a face. 'On our first trip over here we had to visit all the relatives, and every house we went to we had to drink cups and cups of the stuff, even with our meals. I would have killed for a gin and tonic, or a glass of wine!'

Michael laughs. 'You'd never have known it. You'd have been proud of her Anton, the way she behaved. There was my whole family, turning out to look her over, and she had them eating out of her hand in no time!'

'But it was easy,' protests Olivia. 'I liked them.'

She did like them, and she admired them for the kind, if mystified, manner in which they accepted her arrival; the way in which they worried about her comfort, in their efforts to make her feel at home. His mother showed her the garden, asking what plants did her own mother grow, back in Africa? His sisters fingered her clothes – her inappropriate Indian skirts and sandals – and admired her hair, and his father said, 'You'll not be interested in looking at cows now,' and was greatly pleased when she said she was. She did her best to help in the kitchen and went with them to church on Sunday; and at night she and Michael lay together in the creaking wooden bed and talked.

For Olivia, this is perhaps the closest she's ever felt to anyone. She and Michael are bound together by their shared secrets, by the weight of the past – and it's such a brief past, she thinks, for so much to have happened to them. She knows about his earlier loves, the boy who was shot dead in an alleyway, the fear and shame of growing up different in this deeply intolerant society; he knows about Jonathan, and her lost child. And more and more, they are bound by this strange, sweet love, beyond which, for the moment, nothing is expected or desired.

She lies with her head on his shoulder and warms her feet against his. 'What are you thinking?'

'About my father. He told me tonight I'd got myself a lovely woman.'

'Do you feel bad, not telling them the whole truth?'

'No, not really. They wouldn't understand. And anyway, he's right, I have got myself a lovely woman.'

She raises his hand and kisses it. 'And you are a lovely man. We'll always be friends, won't we, whatever happens?'

'Of course.' He squeezes her hand. 'Don't worry about the future, Liv, we'll meet it when we come to it.'

He falls asleep as quickly as a child, but she lies awake in the moonlight and studies him: the eyelashes that lie in a dark fan against his cheek, the softness of his mouth, a vulnerability that catches her throat. How strange it is, she thinks, to be lying here in this war-torn country, and for the first time since she was a small child, feel completely safe.

# 15

The other thing that had surprised Olivia was how quickly she'd come to love the Antrim countryside. Only a month after their return to London at the end of that first visit, Michael had been offered a teaching job in Belfast, so they'd come back to live in the city permanently, in a small house off the Ormeau Road – the house where Anton first visited them.

'Do you remember that little two-up, two down we used to live in?' Olivia asks now, as she drives the short distance from the airport to the seaside town where she's lived for several years.

'I do,' Anton says, 'and that fabulous weekend we spent in Donegal. I was blown away by all that Irishness: the cottage on the edge of the bay, the fields full of sheep ...'

'The duck eggs,' says Olivia.

'Oh God, the duck eggs! And that lake we walked up to in the hills, with the iron-age fortifications on an island in the middle ...'

'And the pub!'

They'd spent the evening in the tiny village pub, where the air was thick with smoke, where someone brought out a fiddle, and a woman sang. Where people said 'South Africa? I've a cousin out there, Fergal Heaney. Would you know the Heaneys?' And when the Garda came around on his bike after closing time, to check that all was quiet, the lights were quickly doused and the handful of drinkers left sat quiet until the all-clear was given, and the evening could be peacefully concluded. The relief of being in a pub where they didn't have to worry about being bombed or shot at was almost more intoxicating than the beer, and when they finally staggered out in the early hours of the morning, they linked arms, with Olivia in the middle, and reeled joyfully home.

The two-up, two down of Olivia's earlier life has given way, all these years later, to the upper storeys of a house in a Victorian terrace, a five-minute walk from the sea. The ground floor belongs to a middle-aged couple, but the rest is Olivia's.

'If you crane your neck, you'll see the lough,' she says, as she shows him the guest room. 'Mine has a better view.'

When he follows her into her room next door, he sees a wide window open onto a view of the sea and the low hills beyond. A ferry is passing, and the white sails of smaller craft fleck the water.

'What a view! I can see why you were so happy to move here – it's a lovely house.'

In the living-room on the floor below, a bay window overlooks the garden. Beside it, there's a door leading into Olivia's workroom, where a trestle table stands beneath another window. Her pens and paints and brushes are neatly stored in pots – disordered in so many other ways, Olivia's tidiness when it comes to her work has always surprised him. He notices the painting at once.

'That's you!' he exclaims. 'It's one of the series Andries du Plessis did.' He studies the painting: the model's pose is abandoned, sensual. He's not sure whether it's just because he knows it's Olivia, and how young she was, that the figure spread out on the glowing fabric looks so vulnerable, or whether it's because the expression in the half-open eyes is slightly wary, at odds with the invitation of the body. 'How long have you had this?'

'It arrived some years ago, just after I moved back here. Out of the blue.'

'What, you mean, in the post?'

'No, it was delivered to the door, by a young woman, apparently. I was out – the neighbours took it in. It had no sender's name or address, and there was nothing else: no letter, no explanation.'

'Do you think it came from Du Plessis himself? Is he still alive?'

'Oh no, it wasn't Dracula, I'm sure of that. I doubt he'd even remember my name – and he'd never have parted with a valuable painting.'

'Then who?'

'I think it can only have been Jonathan.'

'Jonathan Altman?'

'Of course.' Olivia smiles wryly and shakes her head. 'I think he must have bought it soon after we first got together. I remember him mentioning he'd seen it for sale in Simon

Meyer's gallery – Simon was Dracula's agent. I know he was impressed by how much it was worth – I think it made him feel better about me working as a model – and Jonathan was always wealthy, he could have afforded it.'

'But surely he would have told you?'

'Oh no,' she says again, 'not if he was planning to give it to me later. It would have been so like him to buy it as an investment and then put it away, something to give me in the future, to mark a special occasion – even a wedding, if I came up to scratch. But of course, I didn't.'

It's a day for reminiscences. By the time they've walked a couple of miles along the shore, then ducked into a pub to avoid a shower of rain, they've brought each other up to date. Anton has answered her questions about the twins and their families, and about Marie-Claude; he's told her about the chance meeting with the young man who'd sketched her unnoticed at their last meeting, and apologised for forgetting to bring the drawing with him. (Which is less than truthful: the real reason he's left it behind is that he doesn't want to part with it.)

Olivia is entertained by the story: 'Yassine Ayari,' she says, 'I must make a note of his name.'

Back in her flat, she tells him about her most recent visit to South Africa, as they open a bottle of wine and sit down at the table in the bay window to a casserole of lamb and aubergine.

'This is delicious, Liv,' he says. 'You always were a good cook.'

'Marie-Claude's a very good cook too. I remember eating the best duck of my life when I visited you. I'm always surprised you're not fatter!'

Anton laughs. 'Oh, she keeps an eye on me – all things in moderation.'

'It's been a good marriage for you, hasn't it?'

'Yes,' he says. 'It has.'

She pours more wine. 'I had a good marriage too – isn't that funny? I remember that first time you came to visit us, I was so afraid you'd be awkward with Michael, that you wouldn't like each other.'

'I thought he was one of the nicest men I'd ever met,' says Anton.

And Michael had liked him. In the three months that Anton had spent in Belfast, a firm friendship had been established. Over the next two years, Anton came several times to visit them, and Olivia and Michael had travelled once to London, to meet up with him and Marie-Claude, just after they got engaged.

'I'm glad he's marrying her,' Michael had said, as they lay in bed discussing their London weekend. 'They'll be good for each other.'

'Obviously you don't think he's still in love with me? Or possibly you?'

It was one of the things they joked about in private, but Michael said, 'Oh, Anton will always be a bit in love with you, the way I am with Patrick. We see you as basically not quite human: exotic, godlike creatures, briefly lighting up our earthly existences, for which we are duly grateful, but in our hearts, we don't really want anything more because we know that closer contact would probably destroy us!'

'If that bit's in your novel, I think you should delete it,' said Olivia. 'And I very much doubt that Anton sees me as a goddess!' She laughed, then went on, 'I meant to tell you, there's a letter from my mother, they're thinking of taking their lives in their hands and coming over to visit us next year.'

'Well, that's good news! My mum and dad will be thrilled.'

'And Cynthia is pregnant – due around the same time as your sister.'

'Liv,' he reached for her hand. 'I'm sorry, that must be hard for you.'

'Oh well, I'm glad for her, and it's a good thing that both sets of parents are being presented with grandchildren – it will take the pressure off us.'

But the pressures were there, not least what she recognised in herself as a growing restlessness. She'd managed to sell a humorous, illustrated article to a local paper (a series of comic sketches linked with brief passages of prose, about being a foreigner in Northern Ireland) and she had some hope of other work, but it wasn't enough. Michael's energies on the other hand, were absorbed by his teaching job, his writing, and by the search for a publisher for his first completed novel.

And then, on the same day that he finally received a letter from a publisher expressing interest in his book, Michael himself went into town and was blown to a thousand pieces when a bomb being transported across town in an unremarkable grey car went off without any warning.

# 16

'To Michael,' Anton says, raising his glass, and Olivia responds, touching her glass to his.

'Do you still see much of his family?'

'From time to time. His parents died some years ago, and his sister Angela too. But his brother still has the farm, and the younger sister lives in Ballymena. Aunt Edna's also dead, of course.'

It was Aunt Edna, Michael's father's unmarried sister, with whom Olivia had struck up the most surprising bond. She'd often wondered just how much Edna suspected about Michael's sexuality – wondered, to tell the truth, about Edna's own inclinations. Brusque and no-nonsense with everyone else, she'd been remarkably gentle in all her dealings with Michael, and after taking her time about sizing up Olivia, she'd made her liking plain. When Olivia made her father-in-law a birthday card with a cartoon of herself wandering around the farm and causing havoc, it was Edna who had showed it to a friend on the newspaper that bought her first article.

Anton, Marie-Claude and Patrick had all flown over for Michael's funeral (Patrick's presence causing something of a stir). The funeral was in any case a focus of national interest: yet another innocent victim of the Troubles, the grief-stricken parents and young, foreign widow, and the unfolding story of the novel that would now be published posthumously; to have a Hollywood star at the graveside made it international news. Olivia wondered at the time if this was any comfort to Michael's parents. They seemed to have shrunk overnight, standing silent and stunned, their daughters and remaining son beside them – a painfully diminished family group turned in towards each other and away from the rest of the world.

It was also Aunt Edna who in the end had helped Olivia with all the practical details, and Edna who came and fetched her from her little house the day it happened.

'Come home with me,' she said. 'You'll not want to stay here.'

'She was amazing when Michael died,' Olivia says now. 'She sorted out the lease, helped me pack up his things and store what I wanted to keep out at the farm, and she saw me off at the airport. And of course, she was the one who introduced me to Bridie.'

After Michael's death, Olivia had gone home to South Africa for a brief visit. Her parents and sister did their best to comfort her, but the fact that they'd never had a chance to meet Michael made it difficult: they couldn't tell each other the small things they recalled, smile at his remembered quirks, or truly share her grief. And after her years away, even in the troubled north of Ireland, she found the brutal realities of South African life hard to bear. Jonathan Altman, she learned from Suzette, was currently living in Johannesburg, so she ran no risk of seeing him, and Celeste Baker was dancing with a ballet company in America. Apart from Suzette, there was really no-one else she wanted to see.

Back in London, she finds a flat to rent in Earl's Court – and it's here that she answers the door one day to find, to her great surprise, Aunt Edna standing on the doorstep. With her is a small, merry-eyed woman who is introduced to Olivia as 'my very good friend, Bridie'.

'A sort of female leprechaun,' Olivia tells Anton and Marie-Claude, the next time they meet. 'They were over in London for some Women for Peace thing, and took a chance on finding me in. It's the oddest friendship: Edna is Protestant to the core and Bridie isn't just a devout Catholic, she's an ex-nun! Anyway, Edna brought her along because Bridie's written these stories about a philosophical, travelling cat, and she thought I might be just the person to illustrate them. I thought they'd be dreadful, but actually they're really gentle and funny.'

'What's the cat called,' Marie-Claude wants to know.

'Paddycat!' Olivia starts to laugh. 'I could see him straight away: a sort of cross between Puss-in-Boots and Socrates! So I did a couple of preliminary drawings and it seems there's quite a lot of interest in getting them published!'

'Excellent,' Anton says. 'Which reminds me, what's happened to your own philosopher? What's his name – Ludo? You haven't mentioned him lately.'

'Gone back to Berlin,' says Olivia. 'He had an existentialist crisis, which was a relief really – I was getting fed up with all that sitting around in pubs discussing the nature of reality!'

Marie-Claude laughs. 'Oh Olivia! Why are you always attracted to such hopeless men? We need to find you someone sensible, someone with a proper job.'

But in the end, it's Olivia who gets the proper job, or at least one that pays the rent, because Paddycat turns out to be unexpectedly successful. It's partly a question of timing: the stories have been written at the height of the Troubles by a Catholic ex-nun and illustrated by the widow of a young Protestant killed in a bomb blast; it is an irresistible tabloid story. But long before the success of Paddycat, Olivia finds herself briefly famous when Michael's own book is published. Dark Falling – so presciently named – is not quite a coming-out novel, but it certainly deals with a young man's struggles to come to terms with his sexuality in a homophobic and war-torn society. Surprisingly, it turns out to be both a literary and popular success, and the fact that the author will never write another book makes the story doubly poignant.

Olivia is interviewed by several journalists and even invited to take part in a television chat show – and it's at this event that she first meets a man called Frank Fleming. He isn't the host of the show, but he takes it upon himself to fire provocative questions at the other participants (and Olivia in particular) whenever he gets the chance.

'Frank by name and frank by nature,' he says to her afterwards, although in reality, he's anything but. 'I hope I didn't offend you with my questions?'

Olivia, on the point of shaking her head politely, changes her mind and says 'Actually, you did. Michael died two years ago, and I wasn't married to him for very long, but I loved him. And he loved me, whatever other demons he may have had. And I didn't like your stupid dig about white South Africans either.'

'I apologise unreservedly,' says Frank, 'and I really would like to talk to you a bit more. Will you let me buy you a drink? To make up for my crass behaviour? Please?'

He says this with such wistful, boyish, charm that Olivia finds it hard to say no. From their earlier exchanges she's pretty sure that Frank Fleming's engaging, slightly rumpled, exterior hides something a whole lot more flinty, but there's also something undeniably likeable about him. So she agrees to a drink, and before long has to admit that he's surprisingly easy to talk to.

'Actually, we got on really well,' she reports back to Anton and Marie-Claude a few days later. 'He's a political journalist, of course, but he doesn't take himself too seriously – which I have to say makes a pleasant change from Ludo!'

'So, are you going to see him again?' Marie-Claude asks.

'Yes. Dinner on Friday. I feel almost hopeful!'

'Good,' says Anton. 'And if all goes well and you're still together in three weeks' time, bring him to my birthday party.'

By the time Anton's party comes around, Olivia and Frank are spending most of their evenings together. They have neither of them been swept off their feet, but they find each other physically attractive, and stimulating company – which is more,

Olivia thinks, than some can say. And it's because of Frank that she eventually goes to Lisbon, accompanying him on a trip he is making in order to do a piece on the *retornados* – the hundreds of thousands of refugees returning to Portugal from its newly independent African territories.

'Why don't you come along?' he said. 'Portugal's a truly fascinating country – politically-speaking and culturally – and you're bound to like Lisbon.'

As she'd just completed the illustrations for the first Paddycat, and had nothing else very pressing to do, Olivia was happy to agree. She wasn't all that interested in the political situation herself, but from the moment they arrived, she found herself beguiled by the place, the people, their language, food and customs. In the week that they spent there, she filled two sketch-books with drawings, recipes, tips for travellers – all of which became the basis for the first of her travel books, A Traveller's Notes from Lisbon.

Notes from Madrid came next (with the emphasis on local dishes more pronounced) and when, two years later, she and Frank inevitably but amicably parted company, she went on travelling. Sometimes alone, sometimes with Bridie, occasionally with a friend or lover, Olivia's journeys (and Paddycat's terrain) became progressively wider-ranging; and every two or three years, in between the adventures of the feline philosopher, another Traveller's Notes would be published.

It was a way of life that suited her very well. She had her flat in London, company when she wanted it, and if there were times with Anton, Marie-Claude and their boys, or visiting Cynthia and her growing family, when she felt an emptiness in her own life, she also acknowledged that she'd been luckier than most. Above all, she had the freedom to travel where and when she wanted: Rome, Athens, Cairo, Hong Kong – the list grew ever longer. But in 1990 it was somewhere closer to London that drew her, and for the first time in her life, she travelled to Amsterdam.

# 17

It's getting late, but neither Olivia nor Anton wants to end the conversation.

'How's Bridie doing these days?' he asks.

'Crumbling,' says Olivia. 'She's nearly ninety and her eyesight's starting to go. Patrick will be relieved to know the world has seen the last of Paddycat!'

'I don't know why he's always so rude about Paddycat, but he likes your travel books,' says Anton, 'especially the one on Rome. And speaking of books, it's been suggested to me that I might consider writing a biography of Jonathan Altman.'

There's a moment's silence. Then Olivia says 'He died that day we met on the Embankment outside the Courtauld, did you know? I didn't find out for a week or more, I was so taken up with Cynthia. It was a shock.' She pauses. 'Will you do it?'

'I'm not sure. Probably not.'

Anton isn't being quite truthful: in fact, he's very tempted by the commission. It would mean putting his current project on hold, but the fact that Altman is almost certainly going to be awarded the Kani Prize is stoking international interest in him, so he needs to decide quickly. But Olivia has never talked about her time with Altman, and he knows they're on dangerous ground.

'What about you,' he asks? 'Any more Traveller's Notes?'

'Oh, I don't think so. People aren't interested in that sort of book any more.'

This is true: Olivia's books belong to a different time. She specialised in a quirky, alternative angle, searching out the oddities in people and places, including local recipes and scraps of folklore and illustrating them with her trademark humour. They were slim, attractively priced and packaged, and made popular souvenirs and presents.

'Well, I liked them all,' says Anton. 'How many were there in the end?'

'Altogether? Ten. So, which was your favourite then?'

'Amsterdam, of course. Need you ask ...?'

The room is slowly silting up with ghosts: Michael, his parents, Edna, Jonathan – and now the ghosts of their younger selves.

Olivia had known that Anton would be in Amsterdam when she planned her trip. She'd gone round to the de Waal's for dinner one evening and in the course of the conversation, Anton had mentioned that he was planning to go across during the holidays to do some research.

'Amsterdam would be good for one of your books,' says Marie-Claude. 'Picturesque, lots of quirky corners.'

'But not so good from the culinary point of view,' Anton objects. 'Dutch food tends to be rather stodgy.'

'Not all of it – think of the Indonesian influences – and

there are some wonderful local restaurants.'

'Well,' says Olivia, 'I might think about it.' And as so often happens, things seem to fall into place of their own accord: there are cheap flights, a hotel recommended by a friend, and a familiar wave of restlessness, precipitating action. The fact that Anton will also be in Amsterdam is a bonus.

A few weeks later, they meet for dinner in one of the local restaurants mentioned by Marie-Claude. Marie-Claude and the boys are not in Amsterdam: they've gone to France, to visit Marie-Claude's parents.

'And sooner them than me,' says Anton. 'You've never met her parents, have you? They're the French equivalent of that dreadful old grandmother of the Baileys, the one who lived in Muizenburg. The one we visited on the day I lost the kite.'

'Well, it's a piece of luck for me that you're still here,' says Olivia. 'I prefer travelling solo these days, but I never enjoy eating on my own – this is much more fun!'

Olivia is staying in the recommended hotel, Anton has the loan of a friend's flat, and they meet at this halfway point – a traditional, wood-panelled 'eetcafe', where they sit drinking Jenever at the bar while they wait for a table.

'So, what's new?' asks Anton. 'Or should I say, who's new? I don't think I'm currently up to date with your love life.'

'That's because it's currently non-existent,' says Olivia. 'I'm nearly forty-one, and if what my girlfriends tell me is true, once past forty you might as well go into a nunnery. Unless you're married, of course: married women are always in great demand because they're not looking for commitment. Just a bit of excitement to liven up their humdrum lives.'

'I'll tell Marie-Claude,' says Anton. 'She'll be glad to hear it.'

'Have you ever been unfaithful, Anton?' Olivia asks.

'Yes, once,' he answers briefly.

'Does Marie-Claude know?'

'I don't think so.'

'She'd probably be very French about it anyway, as long as you were discreet.'

'Yes.'

'You're not being very forthcoming,' Olivia complains. 'I'm probably your oldest friend, you know. You're supposed to confide in me. I don't have any secrets from you, after all.'

'I don't know about that,' says Anton. 'In fact, for someone as ostensibly candid as you are, I think you probably have a surprising number of secrets.'

The meal is good, and there's a lot to talk about. Nelson Mandela has just been released from his 27 years of imprisonment, the Cold War is ending – for once the future looks almost hopeful – and they prolong the pleasure of being together with more wine than is sensible. By the time they leave the restaurant, Olivia is a little unsteady; she nearly trips as they step out into the street, but Anton catches and steadies her, and then he kisses her. Time halts. 'Come back with me,' he says.

In the morning she wakes in the unfamiliar room and turns to find him already awake, watching her.

'Oh, Anton,' she says.

'Oh, Olivia,' he responds, with a small, rueful smile. 'How do you feel?'

She groans. 'I feel so guilty!'

'I know, I do too. But there you are, we did what we did. It was a long time coming.' He reaches out and strokes her face. 'But if I may say so, my darling Olivia, it was worth the wait.'

'You don't think I should go into a nunnery then?' she asks.

'You're fishing for compliments, but no, I don't. Come here ...'

'Anton.' She stops him. 'We can't ever do this again – we have to agree on that. Marie-Claude is my friend as well. She might be very French about the occasional affair, but disloyalty is different. She wouldn't forgive that.'

Anton closes his eyes. 'Yes, I know. You're right.'

'So, after this, never again?'

He nods.

'And no regrets?'

'No, no regrets.'

'In that case,' says Olivia, 'we might as well make the most of the time we've got left ...'

'So long ago!' Olivia says now. 'It's hard to remember how I felt then.'

But she does remember. She remembers the sick, hollow feeling in her guts as she said goodbye to him on the morning he left to fly back to London. Anton had been part of her life, for so many years: she was accustomed to being his friend, his confidant; to his slight jealousy each time a new man came into her life. What she hadn't foreseen was that she might fall, so unexpectedly, in love.

'We've never really talked about it,' says Anton. 'You did know how hard it was for me to leave you?'

'Was it? Well, I'm glad to hear it. It nearly killed me.'

'Liv!'

She shrugs. 'Oh, I always knew you couldn't have done anything else. You had Marie-Claude, your boys – we would have been destroying their lives, and probably ours too, if I'm honest. But I did feel very ... alone.'

'Oh Liv, I'm so sorry.' He reaches out to take her hand. 'I didn't realise ...'

'I think Marie-Claude did. I didn't see you for a long time, I remember, and when I did finally come round, she was particularly kind to me. Oh well, water under the bridge ...'

For a few moments there is silence while they both think back. There've been so many other meetings down the years: in coffee shops, in wine bars, a conference they were both invited to in Rome, a chance meeting in Edinburgh. Marie-Claude is sometimes there, Olivia often has a new man in tow. She is always open, affectionate, teasing, and Anton is his quiet, contained self. They meet when they are all in South Africa, she occasionally looks after Pierre and Florian, the twins, and from time to time they spend holidays with Patrick in Ascoli Piceno. But only once do they ever share a bed again.

'You never did a Notes from Istanbul,' Anton observes.

'No. Paddycat in Istanbul was enough, I couldn't bear to do any more – and I could never bring myself to go back.'

'Oh Liv!' he says again, but she shakes her head.

'It's all right Anton, I didn't mean to sound so melodramatic. The reason I never went back was because I couldn't bear it not to live up to what I remembered. It was even harder that time to let you go – but I'd probably do the same again. It was a magical place, wasn't it?'

'Oh yes,' he says. 'Indeed it was.'

*

At the time he'd been furious with Marie-Claude for landing him with the job of showing Bridie around.

Olivia had brought her round for dinner, in the course of which Anton had mentioned his new project, a history of the trade routes that passed through Istanbul.

'Istanbul!' Bridie claps her hands in childlike delight. 'Now there's a place I've always longed to visit!'

'Well then, you should go,' says Marie-Claude. 'It's a wonderful city. And Anton is spending so much time there at the moment, he could show you round, if you time it right.'

'Oh, what a marvellous idea!' Bridie's wrinkled face is alight with enthusiasm. 'And now that I think of it, what a good setting it would be for Paddycat. Oh Olivia, we must go! No, no, I'll hear no arguments! This might be my last book, and my only chance to see Istanbul before I die.'

Bridie says the same thing about every journey, but although she's pushing eighty, her stamina is in no way diminished. She is, in Olivia's opinion, as tough as old boots, and will probably still be travelling round the world long after Olivia herself is six foot under. But she likes to present herself as a frail old lady in need of assistance – a useful disguise that has fooled many an unsuspecting local down the years. Later she rubs her hands with glee as she says to Olivia, 'I'm told Turkey's no place for a woman on her own – or even two together – but with dear Anton there, we'll be entirely safe!'

Bridie with the bit between her teeth is unstoppable; so, two months later, she and Olivia arrive at their hotel in Sultanahmet, the lovely old quarter of the city, and are shown to their rooms, which overlook the Bosphorus. But even before she sees the view, Olivia is enchanted. Everything about the place appeals to her, from the softly-spoken young men at the desk, to the Ottoman-style architecture of the building and the litter of kittens playing in the courtyard. Bridie is similarly smitten.

Anton isn't due to arrive for a few days, but a walking tour has been arranged for them, and a trip up the Bosphorus; by the time he does arrive, Olivia and Bridie have accumulated quantities of notes and sketches. Their hotel is close to both the Blue Mosque and Aya Sofya; they've been to see the mosaics and explored the Basilica Cistern; and they've drunk endless glasses of apple tea in shaded courtyards.

'Dear boy!' says Bridie, when they finally meet up. 'It's miraculous!'

Anton laughs and raises his eyebrows at Olivia.

'Extraordinary,' she says. 'I have to keep pinching myself.'

'Well, I'm sorry I won't be able to give you a lot of time, but I thought we could have dinner tonight, and then tomorrow I could take you to Topkapi and the bazaar, if you'd like that?'

Dinner is outside, at a table in a row down one side of a narrow, sloping lane. The restaurant is famous for its fish, and halfway through the meal Olivia, feeling the slightest of movements near her foot, lifts the long, white tablecloth to see, crouched motionless at their feet, three of Istanbul's skinny, hungry, watchful cats.

These cats are everywhere: under the table where they eat their breakfast in the courtyard of the hotel, sitting still as statues in shop doorways; and in the great covered bazaar, in the section given over to books, a display in one window is carefully arranged around a basket in which a mother-cat is suckling her kittens.

The bazaar delights them, as they wander between the endless stalls and alcoves: cave-like spaces crammed with spices, fabric, jewellery, wonderfully patterned tiles and pottery, shoes, clothing, carpets that must surely fly. On all sides they are petitioned, with humour and with charm: 'Come, come in!' 'Lady, let me sell you something that you do not need!' 'Look! Only look! There is no need to buy!'

But buy she does, beautiful bowls in glorious blues and reds, and (guiltily) a pair of coral earrings that she can't resist. 'Look,' says the elderly salesman to Anton. 'How beautiful is your wife!'

'Yes,' says Anton, 'she is.'

They eat lunch on the terrace at the Topkapi Palace, glad to rest before exploring the complex. But after an hour of wandering through courtyards, kitchens, chambers, the harem, Bridie, uncharacteristically, has had enough.

'Sure, I'm all done in,' she says. 'If you don't mind, Olivia dear, I think I need to get back to the hotel and put my feet up. The old tummy isn't feeling too good – I think it's a bit of fasting and an early night for me!'

Olivia accompanies her back to the hotel, but Bridie won't hear of her staying in for the evening. 'I'll be quite all right, my dear. I've everything I need, and I'd be very upset if you stayed in just because of me. A good night's sleep, and I'll be right as rain again tomorrow.'

*

Back in her own room, she showers, rests, then dresses for the evening. At seven o'clock she makes her way up to the rooftop terrace, where Anton joins her.

'You're wearing your earrings,' he says. 'You look wonderful.'

She knows she's looking her best: the earrings are the same red as her silk shift dress, her hair is swept up for coolness, and the silver rings and bracelets she has collected on her travels gleam on her wrists and fingers.

'You look well too,' she says. 'In fact, for two people nearing their half-century, I'd say we look pretty damn good!' She raises her glass to him: 'Here's to the next fifty years! And thank you for such a wonderful day. I keep thinking it can't get any better, and then it does – I mean, just look at that view!'

As the sun sets over the domes and minarets, and the ceaseless traffic on the Bosphorus, the call to prayer rises up into the evening sky. It's almost unbearably beautiful, and it is nine years since Amsterdam.

The waiter brings small plates of meze, they clink their glasses again, and talk as old friends do. Then Olivia delves into her handbag. 'Look: I've been drawing like a demon!'

She hands him a sheaf of sketches and watches as he sifts through them, exclaiming. 'God, these are lovely! I think they might be some of the best you've ever done – will you let me keep one?' Then he looks up. 'Liv! Are you crying?'

'Oh Anton!' There is a sudden raw desperation in her voice. 'I'm so sorry, but I don't think I can do this ... to be here with you in this magical city, on a night like this, and not ...' Her voice cracks as she reaches out to him. Anton says nothing. He raises her hand to his lips and kisses it gently. Then he beckons the waiter, pays for their drinks, and holding out his own hand, draws her to her feet. Together they go down to her room.

As the red silk dress slides to the floor, Olivia thinks, I will pay for this later. But there's nothing she can do now except cling to him like a drowning woman.

At some point she wakes and hears the distant sounds of the river; the ships and boats that pass each other in the night. Moonlight stripes his sleeping face, their naked bodies ... Like tigers, she thinks, and sleeps again. The next time she wakes, he is gone.

# 18

It's not that Anton has forgotten that night in Istanbul, but time has altered his memories – so much of his past life now has this distorted, faded quality. What surprises him is how well he still recalls the feeling of exhilaration he experienced that night – the sense of power and freedom – as he walked back alone through the ancient streets. He felt young, vigorous – the natural heir to all those other conquerors who'd passed that way before him. Now, ten years later, he feels weighted down by age, and slightly the worse for drink.

'I think I always saw you as someone who just took love – sex, I suppose – as and when it came,' he says. 'You were always such a law unto yourself – I thought *I* was the one who had to struggle with conventional bourgeois feelings and domestic ties, while you just went blithely on to the next adventure. How selfish that seems now...'

The remorse he feels is genuine, but it's also tinged with resentment. How could he have known that this affair would be so different for her from all the others? At the same time, he's forced to acknowledge that he never really gave much thought to the possible consequences for her. He'd gone back to his family – to the chains and comforts of his marriage, his children – while she had gone back to, what?

'Liv,' he says, 'I am truly sorry.'

'It's all right,' she says again. 'What doesn't kill you...'

'Is that why you left London?'

'Partly – there were too many opportunities for us to run into each other – but to be honest, I think I'd had enough of London by then, and I still had Michael's family in Northern Ireland. It's funny, isn't it, that three of my happiest – or at any rate, most secure – years were spent in Belfast in the Troubles! And it was a good decision, all things considered.'

What she doesn't tell him is that she saw him once, a year or two after Istanbul, on O'Connell Street. She had taken the train down from Belfast to spend the day in Dublin, to see an exhibition and wander the shops, when suddenly there he was, standing only a little distance away, looking at his phone. She knew immediately that he'd be there to do some research. Marie-Claude could have been with him, but it was more likely that he was alone. If she stepped forward now, he would see her; they would both exclaim at the coincidence, embrace as old friends do, agree to go for coffee or a drink ... And then? Instead, she pressed herself back against the wall, watching as he tapped the phone briefly before returning it to his pocket; forcing herself to stay where she was, motionless in the shadows, as he turned and walked away from her.

*

And for once in Olivia's life, virtue is rewarded. Shaken by this sighting of Anton, she loses the desire to stay any longer in Dublin, and makes her way back to the station, where she takes an earlier train home. It's relatively empty, for a change, and she's lucky enough to have a corner to herself where she can spread her newspaper on the table. The world is at the start of a new millennium and after another decade of bombings, shootings, Bosnia, royal deaths and divorces, not to mention HIV and Mad Cow disease, it seems that today at least the news is mildly optimistic. But even that can't cheer her: she feels sad, alien, rootless – much older than her fifty years. As the train draws in at Newry, she folds the paper, settles her head back against the seat, and tries to sleep. But she's aware that someone has taken the place opposite her, and when she opens her eyes, she sees a man whose face she knows.

'I'm sorry. I was trying not to wake you.'

'I wasn't asleep. Anyway, who on earth could object to being woken by Liam McMahon?'

He gives a small ironic bow. 'You're very kind. Your face is familiar to me too.'

'Olivia Martin.'

'I have your Travel Notes from Paris,' he exclaims. 'And Paddycat! The grandchildren love Paddycat – my stock will go up no end when I tell them I met you!'

She laughs. 'Not nearly as much as mine when I tell my friends I met Liam McMahon! What is someone as exalted as you doing down here with us lesser mortals?' She gestures at the rest of the carriage, which is a bit fuller than it was, but none of the other passengers appears to have noticed that one of Ireland's foremost poets is amongst them.

'I'm mean,' he says. 'Anyway, why would I pay through the nose to travel in First Class when I'm just as comfortable here? And so much more likely to meet an interesting companion?'

She laughs again. 'You may regret it! I'm not a great reader of poetry but I bought your last book after I saw you being interviewed on the BBC, and there are several questions that I'd like to ask ...'

Afterwards, the memory of his voice fills her ears, and she can recall almost every word of their exchange. His face, with its deep-set, tired eyes, is etched on her own mind's eye: a Renaissance face, she thinks, watchful, dark, astute. It's by no means the first time Olivia has experienced an instant liking for a stranger – and enjoyed conversations that have sometimes flowered into unexpected friendship – but this is different. There's an immediate rapport: a warmth and ease between them, a sense of mutual recognition, and (she's mildly ashamed of this) a growing undercurrent of excitement. It doesn't seem possible that the weary emptiness she felt such a short time ago could so suddenly have vanished, but there it is: the first, invisible tendrils of something new have entered the carriage and are threading themselves around her.

From Newry to Belfast they talk – about themselves, about their work, their lives, books, art, the world. He mentions his wife who is an invalid, children who are grown; she tells him about her sister's illness, her childhood in South Africa. It's a country he's never visited, but they find they share a love of music, food and wine, the pleasures of solitary travel. And all the while another, more urgent, conversation is going on between them – one that might be apparent to anyone who cared to look, but nobody does. After all, they're just two unremarkable middle-aged people, talking to each other in a carriage full of passengers intent on their own concerns. But as the train draws at last to a halt, he reaches suddenly for her hands and says, 'Olivia, when and how can we meet again?'

'Olivia?' She's recalled to the present by Anton, who is gesturing at the wine.

'No.' She shakes her head. 'I'm drunk enough, and drink and ancient wrongs are a fatal combination!'

He isn't entirely sure what wrongs she's referring to now. He knows there's still enough of his Calvinist upbringing in him to make him feel that Olivia has reaped no more than she has sown, but he dislikes this disapproving side of himself, and tonight he feels such a wave of sadness for her that he finds himself asking, 'Did you ever wish you'd had children, Liv?'

'Another child, you mean? Oh yes, I wish I'd had the sort of life where it might have been possible for me to have had a child, but that's not how it turned out. And I've no regrets – except that now I wish I'd been brave enough to stand up to Jonathan all those years ago.'

'But he stood by you, surely? I mean, what else could he have done?'

'Oh Anton, that old rubbish about the child I aborted being Joseph Kani's? I never slept with Kani, Anton, not in that sense. The child was Jonathan's.'

'*His* child?' His face is so blank with surprise that she almost laughs. 'But why?'

'Because he gave me no choice. He'd decided I wouldn't

make him a suitable wife, and it would have been equally damaging to his prospects to have had a disreputable wife, or an ex-girlfriend and a bastard hanging about. Anyway, he had someone else already lined up, although I didn't know it at the time.'

'But he told me himself ... well, perhaps not in so many words, but he certainly gave us all to understand ...'

'Well, which version would *you* prefer? To be the man who talked the girlfriend he was planning to ditch into having an abortion, or the one who bravely supported the woman he loved, even though she'd been unfaithful?'

'Liv! Why didn't you tell anyone the truth? Why have you never told me?'

'Because I was humiliated and ashamed. I was ashamed that I'd made such a mess of my life – that I'd been persuaded to agree to something I regretted. And because you've never asked – although, to be fair, I've never wanted to talk about it either.' She sighs. 'You may have forgotten what it was like back then, but your reputation was everything – a woman's, of course, not a man's. If you think about it, even now 'promiscuous' is a word applied almost exclusively to women – or gay men – and in those days, to be an unmarried mother was a disaster ... I think I could have done it though, if I'd had any way of supporting myself, but I didn't. I was so young ...' She closes her eyes for a moment, then looks directly at him. 'It's not as though I'm the only woman it's ever happened to. At least that story about the baby being Joseph Kani's gave me some sort of public kudos, and saved me from the humiliation of everyone knowing that Jonathan didn't think I was good enough for him. And I'm proud that Joseph spent that night with me – I hope to God I gave him some comfort, because he was a better man than any of you.'

The bitterness in her voice shocks him into silence, but then she says 'Oh Jesus, Anton, I'm sorry, I didn't mean to be so unkind. You're my oldest friend and I love you, and whatever you and I have shared was by mutual consent, but Jonathan was different. He caused me the greatest grief in my life, and got away, not just scot free, but with his reputation enhanced. But there you are, that's life, and in the end what does it really matter? I can't deny the good he did for so many people, and God knows it was needed. When you think of what South Africa was like in those days ...'

'*Of course* it matters! For heaven's sake, Liv! Did you never hear from him again?'

'No, not once in all those years. He bought me my plane ticket and that was that. Although he must have kept track of where I was: I'm quite sure he sent me the painting, God knows why, because he could just have quietly sold it.'

'Perhaps it was meant as some kind of peace offering?'

'Or blood money?' She shrugs. 'I think it's unlikely his family knew he had it: he'd hardly have hung it on the wall after he married Rachel – everyone knew it was of me. No, I think he probably held onto it for sentimental reasons, or because it was valuable, and then he saw an opportunity to get rid of it. He was getting older, after all – he might have had a health scare – and maybe he didn't want his family unearthing it when he died. Perhaps it salved his conscience in some way, or maybe it was just an act of uncharacteristic sentimentality. Who knows?'

She reaches out and pats his hand. 'It's all right, Anton. It's true I would have liked to have had a child – a brave, fierce daughter, for preference, who would have told the world to go hang and kicked any man in the teeth who tried to harm her – but I can't really complain: I've had a better life than most, and for the last few years I've been unexpectedly happy.'

'Liam?'

'Yes,' she says. 'And I know what you're going to say: that I'm still with a man who's tied to someone else, who can't acknowledge me openly. The difference is that he would have left his wife long ago if I'd asked him to, but she's been an invalid all the time I've known him, and he has children. I won't cause any more damage to anyone – not if I can help it.'

She reaches out, caps the bottle, and pushes back her chair. 'And now, I think it's time we went to bed. You go on up – I just want to clear a few things here. There are blankets in the chest if you're cold. Sleep well, Anton.' And she kisses him lightly on the cheek.

Anton does not sleep well. Partly it's the drink, which wakes him in the small hours with a dry mouth and full bladder, but mostly it's the new light that Olivia has shed on his hero, Jonathan Altman, and for which he's less than grateful. Because Anton has (of course) already mapped out a framework for his biography; but what he knew – or thought he knew – about Altman has now taken on a somewhat different perspective.

None of this alters the fact that the man had been a powerful agent for change in the old South Africa, often at great personal risk, and had worked tirelessly all his life – not least, in recent years, in the field of women's rights. Anton tells himself that, after all, Altman had the normal human failings, and who knows what any of us might not do when a great deal is as stake. Not that it helps: he feels a deep sad fury on Olivia's behalf, and at the same time he is angry with her for saddling him with this unwanted knowledge. So, tossing and turning, he passes a restless and unhappy night.

# 19

Olivia doesn't sleep much either, but then, she doesn't expect to. In the last year or so, the vague aches and pains that have begun to plague her seem to have grown more insistent, and the medication she takes at night won't mix well with the wine she's drunk; but at least to begin with, the alcohol brings a certain warmth and comfort. As she listens to the spatter of rain against her window, she closes her eyes and wills herself to empty her mind of present cares, to wait for the current of memory to carry her back...

It is ten years ago. It's seventeen hours since she scrawled her number on a piece of paper and gave it to him as the train arrived in Belfast. It's seventeen hours and fifteen minutes since they parted – but she knows he'll ring, and he does.

'Olivia? It's Liam.'

'Liam.'

'Olivia.'

She laughs. 'We can't go on saying Olivia and Liam, over and over! Tell me what you've been doing.'

'Thinking about you, mostly. Going over our conversation ...'

'Me too. Where are you now?'

'Walking along the shore,' he says, 'on the other side of the lough. I'm looking across the water to where I think you are.'

'So near yet so far!'

'I could be across there later this evening,' he says. 'Around eight – if you'd like me to come over, that is?'

'Yes,' she says. 'Oh yes, please come.'

There is so much written about love, about passion, Olivia thinks, and she herself has had more lovers than she can always remember, but nothing has prepared her for this. Always before, some small part of her has remained detached, observing; even with Anton, some instinct for self-preservation kept a tiny corner of her mind aloof. But this time she's lost: suspended in a timeless space between life and death, and if she died now, it would not matter.

'I love you,' he says. 'You must believe me when I tell you that this is different from anything that's ever happened to me before. But it's true: I knew at once – the moment you opened your eyes on the train and looked at me – that I had been looking for you all my life.' He traces her lips, her neck, her breasts. 'Olivia – my beautiful Olivia – please tell me what you're thinking?'

'Much the same as you,' she says. 'That of all the things that have happened in my life, this has to be the most extraordinary.'

And it's true. Love may have come late, but she doesn't doubt for one moment that it has come. She's fifty years old, yet she feels like a child. There's that same tingling excitement, the expectation of magic as a curtain rises, the transfiguring moment when the everyday world is swept away. And although she knows very well that the everyday world is out there, waiting, for the time being she doesn't care.

Everything about him delights her: his hands, the ease with which their bodies fit together, his deep sombre eyes, and his hair, which like hers was once dark and is now patched with silver. There is no other face in the world that she wants to look at as she looks at his, no voice that has ever given her such pleasure. And words, of course, are his most powerful weapon.

Olivia has frequently been less than complimentary about poets: there's one in particular whom she often mimics, an earnest woman whose delivery is so portentous, whose pauses are so long, that Olivia likes to mime the audience nodding off and jerking awake at the start of each new line. She tells him this and he laughs – then slowly, softly, recites the words of some ancient, long-dead lover, reducing her to tears, and shivering delight.

He can't stay the night: his wife is being kept company by a neighbour, and he's promised he'll be home by midnight. But until then they are free to lie in each other's arms and talk, as they will continue to talk down the years to come.

# 20

'Well,' says Patrick, who has turned up at the De Waals' a week or two after Anton's visit to Belfast, 'how was Olivia? Still possessed of boundless energy?'

'Less than usual,' says Anton. 'She'd caught some bug and was having difficulty shaking it off. But then, Olivia, like all of us, isn't getting any younger.'

'Speak for yourself,' says Patrick. 'I consider myself to be in my prime. What about her famous poet? Still keeping her warm?'

'Patrick,' says Marie-Claude, 'is there anyone whose private affairs aren't known to you?'

'One or two,' says Patrick, 'but Olivia and Liam McMahon are an open secret. Not that anyone seems to mind. The wife's been an invalid for years, after all, and they've been terribly discreet: so long as they're sufficiently self-denying and don't go around flaunting any actual happiness, his fans won't mind. The Irish like a bit of suffering.'

'I met him, actually,' says Anton. 'We went out to dinner the night before I left. I must say I liked him very much. And he adores Olivia, that's plain.'

'Did she shed any light on the early years of the sainted Jonathan Altman?'

'A bit, but nothing particularly useful for the book.'

The book, of course, was Anton's excuse for the trip to Belfast: Olivia is his oldest friend, but she was also part of Jonathan Altman's life, and he's at that very early stage of a project where he's considering all the possible avenues and angles.

It was Liam McMahon who'd brought the subject up when Olivia had excused herself and been briefly absent from the table. Turning to Anton, he'd said, 'Olivia tells me you're thinking of writing a biography of Jonathan Altman?'

'Thinking, yes, although I'm not yet sure I'll take it on: he's not my usual field, and he's a rather complex figure.'

McMahon regarded him neutrally. Anton knew he'd be in possession of all the facts regarding Olivia's life, but he gave no sign of any partiality.

'On the other hand,' Anton continued, 'he was a remarkable figure in South African political history. I think I'm probably right in saying that a lot of biographers would have to struggle with even more complex and difficult figures in the Northern Irish context?'

'Indeed,' said McMahon. 'Well, I wish you well with whatever you decide to do. And how have you found things here on this trip? I think it's some time since your last visit.'

After which the conversation turned to other things.

*

Back in London the conversation has also turned, this time to the affairs and fortunes of Yassine Ayari, to the growing interest in his work, and to his upcoming exhibition in New York.

'We must all go over for the opening,' says Patrick.

'Oh, I don't think I want to do that,' says Anton. 'I've got too much going on here.'

'*Of course* you have to be there,' says Patrick. 'After all, you're the one who discovered him, more or less, and a few days off will do you good.'

Marie-Claude uncharacteristically reaches across the table for Anton's hand and says, 'Please come. It would be so nice for us all to be there together.'

And it occurs to Anton, belatedly, that he's neglected Marie-Claude of late. He's been so absorbed in the Altman story that he hasn't really been paying much attention to her, but he sees now that she's looking slightly weary. Or maybe it's something else? – a faint air of resignation, even sorrow – and he wonders suddenly if it's something to do with Yassine; if Ayari – like Olivia, who burned across his own sky so long ago – has not perhaps had the same effect on his wife? Who knows what there's been between them? He's a young man with an unusually compelling physical presence, and a manifest ability to make the most of every opportunity. Anton, who up until now has seen him mainly as the object of Patrick's undisguised lust, now wonders whether Marie-Claude hasn't also been seduced? He'll never ask her, of course, but he decides then and there that he will go to New York to support her (and possibly Patrick too) as they see their protégé blaze off to new horizons.

Some half-remembered words of poetry float into his head, something about children, whose 'souls dwell in the house of tomorrow, which you cannot visit' – Tagore? Gibran? He thinks of his two sons, Pierre and Florian, already launched on their own lives and careers and moving inexorably away. He also thinks – fleetingly – of the soul of Olivia's unborn child, before consigning all such pointless sentiment to the dustbin of memory. In the end there is only this moment now, his wife and his friend beside him, one more glass of wine to be drunk as plans are made; and in the morning, work to be done on the book.

*

Olivia wakes to the sound of her phone. It's Liam.

'If you could go to one place in the whole world for two weeks, just you and me together, where would it be?'

Cities and countries flash through her mind: Venice? New York? South Africa?

'Greece,' she says.

'Why Greece, particularly?'

'Because I went there only once, and I've always wanted to go back. Because I've never been to Greece with a lover. And because you are a poet.'

'Well then,' he says, 'Greece it is.'

'And how is this going to happen?'

'Nuala. She's offered to have Teresa for a couple of weeks so that I can have a break. She told me to be sure and take myself off somewhere where I wouldn't run into friends or family, where I could have peace and quiet, and a proper holiday.'

There is a little silence, then Olivia says, 'God bless Nuala.'

*

Liam and Olivia have had holidays before: one autumn they went to a friend's cottage in Mayo for a couple of nights; once or twice they've managed to be invited to the same conferences, and to stay in the same hotels. They've had stolen nights in Dublin, London, Edinburgh, but it's always been surreptitious, hurried; never before have they had two whole weeks to themselves.

Nuala Harold is Liam's sister. Liam has always talked to Olivia about his family, but photographs and anecdotes have had to take the place of physical meetings – there have been no shared family occasions. She's searched the internet though, and there's very little she doesn't know about his wife, children, sisters, brothers. Their names and faces are committed to her memory; occasionally she hears one of them mentioned, or sees a face she knows in the street, but she's careful to give no outward sign of recognition.

And then, one day a few years ago, when she was at some literary event with Bridie, a woman approached her and said 'I'm Nuala Harold. I think you know my brother, Liam McMahon?'

'Of course,' says Olivia. 'You're very like him.'

Nuala Harold has a copy of Paddycat in Paris, which she asks Olivia to sign for her granddaughter.

'These books have been great favourites in my family down the years,' she says. 'Do you have children of your own?'

'No,' Olivia answers, 'just nieces and nephews. I do sometimes think how odd it is that both Bridie and I are childless but have collaborated all these years on children's books.'

For no reason that she can put her finger on, she's suddenly sure that Nuala Harold knows she and Liam share more than their literary interests: perhaps she's glimpsed them somewhere together or understood from something in his face or voice that they are lovers, have been lovers now for several years. At the moment she's watching Olivia with the same neutral, guarded expression that her brother so often wears in public.

'I think they're starting to serve coffee,' says Olivia. 'Shall we go and get a cup?' And they move across the room together, talking.

A week or two later they ran into each other again, in the foyer of the cinema where they had gone, separately, to see the same French film. They fell into conversation, sat beside each other in the auditorium, and afterwards shared a glass of wine: the start of a strange, rationed friendship, in which her relationship with Liam was never mentioned, and no intimacy ever sought that could be seen as disloyal to his wife or children. Probably she had satisfied herself that Olivia had no intention of causing any trouble; but whatever her reasons – her liking for Olivia, love and sympathy for her brother – it was after this second meeting that she started inviting her sister-in-law, from time to time, to stay with her. Widowed, with her own children grown and gone, and with a convenient ground-floor bedroom, Nuala had suggested to Teresa that an occasional change of scene would do her good. It made sense too, that when Liam was away, lecturing or making some literary appearance, Teresa should come to her, rather than ask a neighbour or one of the children to look after her.

*

Marie-Claude brings the official invitation to Yassine Ayari's New York opening into the kitchen, where Anton has just poured a glass of wine, and together they toast their protégé's future. Anton is feeling unusually content: the Altman project has fired him with an energy and enthusiasm that he hasn't felt for some time, and he's done another good day's work. After so many years of writing from the lofty perspective of two or three centuries' distance, he's finding the immersion in the more recent past utterly absorbing. Besides, he knew the man personally, and those turbulent years were ones that he lived through himself; there is also his conviction that, whatever Altman's personal failings, the man deserves a good biography. It's a little uncomfortable for him, given Olivia's revelation, that Altman's image is founded on such spotless integrity, his lifelong devotion to truth, justice and equality, but the fact remains that he was one of the few white heroes of the struggle. And who has not, at some point in their youth at least, done something that they later regretted? The solution is to keep the personal stuff to a minimum – which isn't hard because in Altman's case it's not particularly interesting. He had an apparently faithful marriage, fathered two children, and a few years after his first wife's death, married a widowed colleague. From the family research that Anton has been able to do, there don't seem to be any skeletons in the closet.

David Altman is the younger of Jonathan's children. He'd been in London for a few days recently, and Anton's publisher had set up a meeting between them, a meeting that takes place over lunch in Highgate.

David is a geologist, a likeable young man in his early thirties. He's here on unspecified family business but talks easily about his father. No, he can't remember ever feeling neglected by him, despite his heavy political involvement. But then, he and his sister just took it for granted that it was their mother's role to be there all the time; that she would attend the parents' meetings and school events; would organise their birthday parties and tuck them into bed at night.

'It's a bit different for fathers these days!' He laughs. 'God forbid I should miss a concert or a sports day! Looking back, I think my own father was probably fairly ruthless about compartmentalising his life, but when he did spend time with us, he gave us his full attention. And once we were old enough to realise what he was involved with, I think we were very proud.'

In the course of their conversation, Anton brings up several names, some of which David remembers well, others less so. But when Anton says 'I don't suppose he ever mentioned Olivia Martin, did he? She was a mutual friend in our university days,' David says, 'Yes, I know the name, but I've never met her. I think my parents both knew her before I was born but lost touch when she left South Africa. Funnily enough, I had to deliver something to her once. I was going over to Belfast for a conference and Dad asked me to take a parcel and get it sent on.'

'How intriguing. Do you know what was in it?'

'Oh, I think it was a painting of some sort. I didn't see it, it was well wrapped-up, but he'd come across it soon after my mother died, when he was clearing out an attic or office: it may have belonged to Mum. Anyway, Dad thought it was something she might like to have. I don't think there was any mystery about it, he just thought it would be safer to send it with me – and cheaper! And as it happened, one of my colleagues at the conference offered to drop it off for me: I asked her about the address, and it turned out she lived close by. I was pushed for time, so I was grateful.'

*

Which explained the provenance of Olivia's painting. He thinks it highly unlikely that David's mother had bought or been given the painting: what woman would want to keep a constant, immortalised, reminder of her husband's previous lover? No, it seems obvious that Altman had, as Olivia suspected, bought the painting during their time together. He must have kept it all those years, and after his wife's death, taken the opportunity to send it to Olivia, although just why he should have done so will remain a mystery. Perhaps selling it would have risked giving rise to ripples of speculation, to the revisiting of a past best left buried; perhaps in the end it was simply a gesture prompted by the remembrance of love. It will be interesting to see what Olivia thinks; he should in any case get in touch with her soon, to tell her he's accepted the commission, and that Altman's biography is well underway. If he does it now, she'll have plenty of time to come to terms with his decision before the work is published.

As it turns out, Olivia saves him the bother, because a few days later she rings. She's making a new will, she says, and wants him to be one of her executors.

'Don't you want to choose someone younger?' Anton asks. 'We're the same age, after all, and women always last longer – you're bound to outlive me!'

'I sincerely hope so,' says Olivia, 'but for the time being, I'd like to put you down. Is that ok?'

'Of course. And I'm glad you rang, because I've been meaning to get in touch, to tell you that I've decided to take on Jonathan Altman's official biography after all.'

There's a little silence.

'Liv? I'm sorry, I know it's a painful subject for you ...'

'No, no, it's fine. It's your work, and there'll be all sorts of books written about him now, I suppose.' She gives a short laugh. 'Women may live longer, but by and large it's the men who get remembered! Still, I'm sure you'll do it very well.'

'Thank you,' he says.

He finds that he can't after all bring himself to tell her about the painting, or that he's met Altman's son; instead, he says, 'Did you get your invitation to Yassine Ayari's exhibition?'

'Thank you, yes, and I'd love to be there, but unfortunately the date clashes with other plans: I'll be in Greece with Liam – but I'll expect a full report when we all get back.'

They exchange a few more brief words, she sends her love to Marie-Claude, and to Patrick, then she says goodbye and rings off.

# 21

Olivia and Liam fly separately to Gatwick, where they're booked in overnight at the same hotel; in the morning, they fly side by side to Greece – to the southern end of the Peloponnese peninsula, where the port of Kalamata lies in the first of two gulfs between three long fingers of land reaching down to the Mediterranean. Olivia, whose only previous trip to Greece had taken her to Athens and on to the Aegean islands, and Liam – who has never been here either – are both looking forward to seeing a part of the country that promises so much (a wild and beautiful landscape drenched in mythology and history) but with the added attraction of being off the usual tourist track.

Their hotel is just outside the centre of the town. There are palm trees in the garden, a long, curved strip of beach, and a balcony that overlooks the silken waters of the bay. That first night they eat at the water's edge: plates of meze, cool white wine. Then they wander hand in hand along the shore. It's not yet high season and the only other guests they meet seem to be mostly Greek or Russian. No-one approaches or shows the slightest interest in them, and they are free to walk, talk, eat and drink together, and to wake beside each other in the morning.

Right from the start, time becomes curiously elastic – it seems to stretch out, then stop for long still spaces, before slowly beginning to snake away again. They eat breakfast on their hotel terrace, read or swim in the pool or in the sea, and walk into the town to wander through squares and alleys, through rich, shadowy churches, and along a waterfront lined with shops and cafes. In the languorous afternoons they lie naked on their bed, and in the evenings they explore the local restaurants and bars.

It's in one of these bars that they first hear about the ancient ruins in the mountains up behind the town. The proprietor gives them the name and number of a driver – a young man who turns out to be his nephew, and whose English puts them to shame, as does his good-humoured and dignified explanation of his job. He's actually a qualified civil engineer, but in the current economic climate he can't find work, so he's come back from Athens to help his uncle in the tiny bar and earn what he can as a taxi driver when there are tourists to employ him. His name is Achilles.

Achilles drives them up into the hills, to a place where the remains of temples, amphitheatres and pillars are scattered down the steeply sloping mountainside in astonishing profusion. There are no tourists, no insistent guides, or sellers of souvenirs – just one old man in a little hut to whom they pay the few coins that gain them entrance, and a small party of archaeologists working on one of the sites. It's silent, sunny, and infinitely peaceful.

They take their time exploring, climbing back up slowly because Olivia has lately found herself getting breathless after exercise. 'God, I'm unfit!' she says, as they sit down on a stone bench in the shade of an old, twisted tree. 'I'll have to join a gym when we get home!' But Liam says, 'You should see a doctor when we get back: I think you've lost weight.'

'Don't fuss, Liam, I'm fine. It's just a legacy of that bug I picked up last year. It takes longer to get over these things when you're older.'

Liam himself, although three years older than Olivia, has the gnarled, lean frame of a manual labourer – unfairly, as she likes to point out, since he's spent most of his life doing nothing more strenuous than write poetry.

'All the same,' he says, 'you shouldn't be getting breathless.'

She pats his hand. 'What a worrier you are! I'll have a check-up when we get back.'

What she doesn't say is that she cancelled a doctor's appointment just minutes after he'd phoned to tell her about Greece. For one thing, she didn't want anything interfering with the holiday; but the other reason is that she knows from experience that one appointment can all too easily lead to another, to unpleasant tests and x-rays and further investigations. She's seen too many people go down this route already, and although she has a good idea of the sort of thing she might be looking at – well, who hasn't got the seeds of something nasty lurking in their body by her age? Why find out about it any sooner than you have to?

All the same, she's begun to put her affairs in order, just in case – shredding, sorting and ruthlessly disposing of accumulated odds and ends. It's a small accumulation: Olivia has never been sentimental, and she's moved house far too often to have built up the collections of keepsakes and memorabilia that clog the arteries of so many of her friends' homes. But there are photographs, diaries and letters, and a battered book she's had for forty years. In this are written or pasted lines of poetry and prose; quotations, sketches, newspaper cuttings; the Order of Service for Michael, and for others. Folded carefully at the back, are the poems that Liam has written for her eyes alone.

She thinks she might have intended it, at the start, as a travel diary: the very first thing written in it, in the round, firm hand of the young Olivia, is a quotation in French. One of her (many) youthful pretensions was that she spoke better French than she did. '*Heureux qui comme Ulysse a fait un beau voyage*'. Well, she has made a good journey, all things considered, and like Ulysses she has, against the odds, survived. With any luck, she'll go on doing so.

Here in Greece, it's so much easier to become resigned to whatever the future might hold. It's something to do with the cleansing quality of light and sea, she thinks; with the vast presence of history, which reduces to a pinpoint the importance of the present. Sitting next to Liam and looking out across the tumbles of ruined stone, Olivia has a sudden vision of herself as a tiny, ant-like figure in an unending procession stretching back to the dawn of time. She breathes in the dry, aromatic air, feels the warmth of the sun soaking into her bones, and is grateful for the impervious, timeless beauty of the land. The land doesn't care about birth or death, the armies that have come and gone, the refugees, the dispossessed, the bodies of drowned children that will continue to wash up on the pristine shores; the olive trees will go on bending in the wind, the waves will keep breaking and receding, and although the soil and rocks of this mountain slope can from time to time convulse and quake, by and large, all this will still be here in a thousand years to come – or so she hopes.

Now she says 'I think I'm beginning to buckle under the weight of history. Is it time for a drink?'

So they make their way back up to the small, charming village, where Achilles leads them to the local taverna, and a meal of aubergines, tomatoes, olives, bread and resin-tinged wine.

He raises his glass and says 'Yamas!' then follows it up with some words in Greek, to which Liam responds.

'Your husband speaks good Greek,' Achilles tells Olivia. 'I think it is because he is a poet. If I may say so, I am greatly honoured to be sharing a meal with so famous a man.'

'That's very kind,' says Liam, 'and I'm not that famous really, but all the same, I'm hoping no-one else will know who I am.'

Achilles holds up a palm. 'Of course. You are here to get away from everything, I understand. My lips are sealed.'

Liam laughs, reaching out to clasp his hand. 'Thank you, my friend, we're very grateful. And if you can spare us a bit more time over the next week, there are some other places that we'd like to visit.'

Not only is Achilles free, he's full of suggestions and recommendations, and they are only too happy to put themselves in his hands. Accordingly, he picks them up a day later, soon after breakfast, and they drive south into the Mani, along the ribbon of road that winds between mountainside and sea.

The road turns, climbs inland, past olive groves, ancient stone towers, hamlets, churches – and then, 'Kardamyli,' says Olivia, reading the road sign. 'Could we stop there? It's the home of my favourite travel writer – Patrick Leigh Fermor,' she adds, for the benefit of Achilles.

'Of course. I know the name well,' he replies. 'A true friend of Greece.' And they turn towards the sea again, and down into the little village of Kardamyli, where they stop just long enough for Olivia to pay homage to the memory of the young man who walked from the Hook of Holland to what was then Constantinople, all those years ago; to look out across the water then wander back along the length of the main street. Olivia buys honey, a bowl, a little cork and pottery olive tree; Liam buys a bookmark.

This is the country of the fortified tower houses of the Maniots. As they climb into the hills they pass these tall stone structures again and again – honey-coloured and forbidding. There are other villages, a little square where Achilles insists on buying them coffee, a Byzantine church with fading frescoed walls; then, on the far side of the Taygetus mountains, they turn back north to Sparta. 'Boring,' says Achilles, 'I will take you somewhere better …' and he drives on to the archaeological site of Mystra, where he drops them off at the upper gate, promising to meet them an hour later at the bottom.

Looking out across the great sweep of the valley and distant blue hills, and – dropping steeply away below them – the tumbling Byzantine ruins of the palaces, churches, monasteries and medieval houses that made up the town, Olivia sighs with pleasure as she links her arm through Liam's.

'How extraordinary!' she says. 'Had you heard of this place before now?'

'I had,' he replied, 'but I'd no idea of the scale. Will an hour be enough, I wonder?'

In the end the descent, along winding stone alleys, takes them considerably longer. There are so many great shadowy chambers to enter, courtyards and archways that give on to vistas of startling beauty, so many photographs to take. By the time they eventually rejoin Achilles (peacefully reading in his car) Olivia feels as though she has been on a carousel ride through centuries of history.

Achilles is delighted with their response to Mystra, and to their exclamations of pleasure as he drives them back westward over the dramatic Langádha pass. And he has one last suggestion to make when he drops them back at their hotel: there is a small local restaurant within walking distance, he says, hidden on the curve of the hill behind them, where they will have the best fish of their lives if they care to eat their dinner there.

The restaurant, as far as they can make out, is run by two brothers, and consists of a dozen rough wooden tables set out beneath the trees, with a glorious view out across the bay. There's a fairly rudimentary kitchen, basic toilet facilities, and a shed housing tanks of mysterious fish. They know the names of none, just point at whatever finny, undulating creatures take their fancy, then sit with wine and bread and a bowl of olives, while the violet evening falls around them, and their meal is cooked.

The food, when it comes, is as unpretentious as it is delicious. The only other guests are an elderly Greek couple, and two silent, solemn men who could be Scandanavian, but as they say so little, Olivia can't be sure. It's hard to believe, sitting here, that in Athens there are riots and protests against the new austerity laws; that chaos is looming. As she looks out across the limpid water – as the sea turns to silver and distant lights spring up in the darkening hills – she gives a long, drawn-out sigh.

'What is it?' Liam asks.

'I was just wishing we could stay here forever and never go back. It's been such a perfect day.'

He gives her his slow smile and continues chewing.

It's strange, she thinks, how characteristics that would infuriate her in anyone else, in Liam do not. He is frugal to the point of parsimony; he can be touchy, quick to see prejudice, condescension; and he eats more slowly than anyone she's ever met. Yet all these things in him are restful, known, endearing. Perhaps it's because she herself is getting older, slower? Would she have loved him as much if she'd met him thirty years ago? She doesn't know. All she knows is that she's grateful that she met him when she did; that when she's with him, she's at peace.

She lifts his hand now and turns it to kiss the pulse on the inside of his wrist. 'I hope you know how happy I am, how very happy you have made me?'

'And you me,' he says. 'And you me.'

# 22

Olivia likes the Greeks: they're the sort of independent, passionate people she greatly admires. She ticks off some of their excellent qualities on her fingers, one by one. 'Warm, hospitable, hard-working, stoic,' she says. 'Not afraid of life or death.'

'Disputatious,' says Liam, 'and bloody-minded, but wonderful writers and philosophers.' (They are both slightly drunk.)

'More importantly, they understand the supreme importance of food and drink,' says Olivia. 'Oh my God, that was delicious!' She leans back, licking her fingers.

They're back in the little hillside restaurant, for the third time. Of all the places that have made such an impression on her, this is perhaps the one that delights her most. It's partly the setting – the canopy of branches overhead, the sea below – and partly the food (Achilles was right: she has never eaten better fish) but mostly it's the tranquillity that encloses them. There is no noise, no rush, no sound of traffic.

Afterwards they walk back along the beach. Ripples of water curl slowly towards them, frothing and dying, again and again; the sea is oiled with light and bounded by the dark, encircling hills, and above it all is the impervious, star-filled sky.

She stops suddenly. 'I want you to promise me something,' she says. 'If I die before you, I want you to promise that my ashes will be scattered on the sea. I don't care where, just so long as they're washed out to sea – then I can hope that at least some part of me will fetch up here again, some day.'

'We've years yet,' says Liam. 'We'll come back before we die, as often as we can. But yes, I do promise.' He stands in silence for a moment or two, gazing out to sea, then turns to face her. 'On the other hand, I can't imagine that life will ever be better for either of us than it is at this moment. Maybe we should just call it a day right now, and swim out together – what about it, Olivia? Shall we trust to the gods to turn us into waves, or dolphins?'

Beneath the humour of the words, she hears an undercurrent of fear, the prescient knowledge of grief, but she answers lightly: 'The trouble is, I've never trusted any gods – least of all Greek ones. They'd be more likely to turn us into crabs, and we'd end up back there in the kitchen, being boiled for dinner. Or one of us would drown and the other wouldn't.'

'You're probably right,' he says, and makes the sound that is so much his, somewhere between a laugh and a bark. 'Besides, we've still got two full days – we wouldn't want to leave before we've had our money's worth.'

On their last night in Greece they lie, propped against pillows, the doors onto the balcony open to the night and the sounds of the sea, and talk into the small hours. Liam never speaks much about his work – indeed, he maintains that until he met Olivia, he had never spoken much at all – but he wants her to know that he has been writing for some months now, a series of poems that are for her, and her alone.

'But you've written poems for me before,' she says. 'I have them all tucked away in a book.'

'Those were private poems,' he replies. 'These are intended for publication, in time.'

She takes this to mean when Teresa is no longer alive. She knows, because Liam has told her so, that he loved his wife; that they had, by and large, a happy marriage. From the photographs she's seen of Teresa in her youth, Olivia thinks she would probably have liked her: there's a warmth, a merriment, in her expression, and great tenderness in the pictures taken with their children. But she's also a woman of deep religious conviction, unbending in her attitudes to marriage and fidelity. Perhaps her illness has made her less tolerant of the weakness of others – for so long now, she's been uncomplaining in her acceptance of the disease that has slowly destroyed her: she believes nothing is sent that cannot be endured, and that her suffering will be redemptive; but the battle has consumed her and left very little room for anything else. What remains for Liam is not love, but duty, and the memory of love.

'What about the rest of the family?' Olivia asks.

'The children? Sure, they're practically middle-aged themselves: old enough at any rate to know that nothing is ever black or white. I'm pretty certain they all know that my life has changed in the last years, but as long as I don't do anything to hurt their mother, they'll say nothing ... they were always closer to her. And God knows the grandchildren won't give a toss!'

'Will you show me what you've written, when we get back?'

'Not yet,' he says. 'When it's done. I just want you to know that I have never loved anyone as I love you, that you have altered my whole existence, and that I can no longer imagine my life without you.'

She closes her eyes, and he whispers, 'Olivia, sweetheart, don't look so sad: we'll come back here again, I promise.'

'Oh Liam, I hope so.'

She waits until he falls asleep, then climbs carefully out of bed. On their little balcony, she leans on the rail and looks out at the dark still sea. If it were not for Liam, she would feel that she herself has lived quite long enough, and she's never been afraid of death, only the painful, long-drawn-out procedures that so often precede it. It's something they've talked about often enough: they're at that age when half their friends seem to have been diagnosed with one cancer or another, dementia, heart disease, Parkinson's – the list is endless – and Liam knows Olivia's view that there's too much medical intervention these days, that quality of life is always preferable to quantity. But she's no illusions about the difficulties that would face him if her health deteriorated. He's not a man given to self-pity or despair, but to have an ailing lover as well as a wife who is a chronic invalid would be enough to tip anyone into a pit of guilt, grief, divided loyalties ... And anger, she thinks, because it's their unspoken expectation that one day, sooner rather than later, Teresa's long battle will be over, and they'll be free to spend their last years together.

Olivia shakes herself. Too much imagination, that's always been her problem; yes, she may have some health problems starting to bother her, but whatever lies ahead, there'll be time enough to think about it when they're home in Belfast. And turning back into their room, she eases herself gently in beside Liam, and wraps her arms around him. This is safety, love, contentment. Let the future take care of itself.

In the morning, they eat breakfast as usual on the terrace, feeding scraps to the thin, quick cats that wait hopefully nearby. (Olivia is reminded of her long-ago visit to Istanbul.) Then, reluctantly, they say goodbye to the waitress they have come to know.

'You'll come back soon,' the woman says, with smiling certainty.

But perhaps the gods that Olivia has never held in much regard have seen what lies in wait, and decided to do her one last favour, because – while Anton, Marie-Claude and Patrick are caught up in the New York bubble of excitement that surrounds Yassine Ayari and the exhibition that everyone is talking about – the little bus that carries Olivia and Liam along the narrow, twisting road back towards the airport, has an unexpected collision with a hapless Greek goat, and veers off the road and down the hillside.

She just has time to see the flaring, yellow eye as they round the corner, the shaggy black pelt flying up into the air, and the blue sky wheeling overhead; then rock and earth race up to meet them and the screen goes blank.

# 23

The path directly below the cottage runs from west to east along the southern shore of the lough. The cottage itself is buttressed on one side by the high walls and hidden gardens of a much older house; on the other it's flanked by an overgrown plot with gates that have been locked for decades, and a couple of bungalows not yet picked off by hovering developers. But most passers-by don't notice the landward side: they're too busy looking out to sea, where the unending procession of ships and ferries passes, where at this time of year, lights prick the darkness early on the far side of the bay. On this particular evening, there aren't many people about and anyway, no-one pays any attention to the peeling gate or shallow steps that lead up to the cottage, itself set well back from the path and partly hidden by trees. But a little breath of wind runs suddenly along the branches, rustling the leaves that frame a lighted window. Or perhaps it's a passing ghost? Certainly, a cat keeping guard on the wall arches its back, and hisses.

The ghost, if there is one, will see through the window into a low-ceilinged room where a wood fire burns. Above the fireplace hangs a painting – indistinct at this distance, but closer inspection will show a young girl lying naked on a vividly coloured cloth. Two people are standing in the window, a man and a woman. The man, who is pouring wine for his companion, has the slightly unkempt look of someone who lives a solitary life – either that or he doesn't care about his appearance. His face is shadowed; his hair, still thick but striped with white, is uncombed and grazes the collar of an ancient jacket. The woman, on the other hand, is elegant – no longer young, but dark-haired, burnished.

'Do you walk much?' asks Marie-Claude, nodding towards the coastal path, a section of which can be seen from the window.

'Every day. It was one of the reasons for buying this place.'

'It's a beautiful part of the world,' she says. 'You were lucky to find somewhere as tranquil as this so close to Belfast.'

'Indeed,' Liam responds. 'I am fortunate.'

It's also close to the spot where he eventually consigned Olivia's ashes to the sea, and he likes to think that such small fragments of her as have not yet found their way back to Africa, to Greece – to one or more of a dozen other favoured places – might still swirl and lap against this shore.

There was no great fuss and furore after the accident. If Liam had died it would have been a different story, but Olivia's fame had been fleeting, and she was of little interest to the outside world. At any rate, no-one remarked – or not for long – on the fact that the injured foreign poet and the woman who died were both from Northern Ireland and might possibly have known each other. There were a couple of brief obituaries (the Guardian's was the longest) but Olivia's one-time boyfriend and fellow-traveller – the journalist Frank Fleming, who would undoubtedly have sensed a story – was also dead, killed in Iraq several years before. If anyone outside their friends and family had an inkling of the connection, they kept the suspicion to themselves. Besides, it was an unusually eventful year: earthquakes and tsunamis vying for attention with assassinations, scandals and an Arab revolution, and then another royal wedding to enjoy, before the endless cycle of natural and unnatural disasters resumed; before the world spun relentlessly on.

'How is your leg now?' Marie-Claude asks. She's seen that he still limps, although the crutches he was on for several months after the accident are no longer in evidence.

'Better, thank you – at any rate, no worse than the rest of me. What it is to find oneself suddenly an old crock!' He smiles at Marie-Claude. 'You, on the other hand, appear to have the secret of eternal youth!'

Marie-Claude touches her glass to his. 'We Frenchwomen have secret potions, passed on to us by our mothers. Didn't you know?' She laughs, then turns towards the painting hanging above the fireplace. 'I've never seen this before, although Anton has told me about it. We were all children when we first met, you know ...' And she recounts the story of the kite being chased in vain across the beach.

Liam can picture the scene – it would make a good painting too, he thinks. 'She wasn't much more than eighteen when that was painted,' he says.

Marie-Claude nods. 'But he caught something that people didn't always see: that mixture of vulnerability and bravado. Anton was right, it's an extraordinary portrait.'

Anton himself has gone to collect Marie-Claude's cousin Patrick from the nearby airport. It's typical of Patrick that on hearing they were planning to visit Liam McMahon to mark the second anniversary of Olivia's death, he had written to McMahon and engineered an invitation.

'I hope you don't mind that my cousin asked to join us,' Marie-Claude says.

'Not at all,' says Liam. 'I've seen him often enough on stage and screen, I'll be delighted to meet him in the flesh. And I understand he had a soft spot for Olivia.'

'We all did,' says Marie-Claude. 'She had a great gift for life, for love – but you of all people know that.' There's a pause before she adds that it's hard to accept that someone who was so very alive is no longer here. 'Or perhaps she is,' she says. 'What do you think?'

'Oh, for me she's very present,' he says. 'Not in the ghostly sense, but in my mind's eye. I still talk to her all the time.' It's an odd relief to admit this. 'And this house isn't far from where she used to live. After my wife, Teresa, died, I moved over to this side of the lough – I like to imagine she's sometimes with me on my walks.'

'Teresa or Olivia?' She raises an eyebrow at him, and there is a moment's shocked silence. Then he throws back his head and laughs.

'Now that would be something!' he says. 'The poet walking with both the shades of the wife and mistress keeping pace! But perhaps you think that would be my just desserts?'

'Not at all,' she says. 'I wouldn't presume to judge. We all have difficult choices to make. I think most of us just try to do as little damage as we can.'

'I can't say I behaved very well when Teresa died.' It's out of character for him to speak so openly, but Marie-Claude is easy to talk to. 'After Greece, I was in hospital for weeks, and glad to stay there.' He remembers how grateful he was for those weeks: for the distance from his wife, his family, and the world – how he welcomed the physical pain, the drugs that helped keep grief and guilt at bay. But grief and guilt were biding their time, of course, waiting patient as animals in the shadows.

'When I got home and found Teresa was finally dying as well,' he goes on, 'I was so filled with rage, I was nearly demented. Not because I'd missed the chance to comfort her at the last – my wife, after all, the mother of my children – but because she'd won. She had outlived Olivia. And all the virtue was stacked on her side, of course: she was the one who was faithful to the end. She had the church packed with mourners, the flowers, the speeches...' (And the sorrowing husband in a wheelchair, he thinks, like a bad movie.) 'Does that shock you?'

'No,' she says. 'It's entirely understandable. But Teresa was your wife, as you say: it was the least she deserved. Anyway, Olivia would have hated all that fuss.' She smiles at him. 'Don't be too hard on yourself: you did the best you could, in circumstances that can't have been easy. And speaking for Anton and myself, we were very glad when you came on the scene. You brought her great joy.'

'Thank you,' he says.

She touches her glass to his. 'To Olivia – and Teresa!' Then she cocks her head: 'I think I hear the car coming back.'

*

But when the door opens to admit Anton and Patrick, Liam sees that someone else is with them: a younger, dark-skinned man who waits, with the composed grace of a dancer about to step onstage, while Marie-Claude embraces her cousin, and introduces him to Liam, before turning to his companion.

'Yassine!' she says. 'Patrick didn't tell us you were coming with him!'

'A stroke of fortune!' says Patrick, blithely unconcerned that he has brought an uninvited guest, on a solemn occasion, to the home of someone he's never actually met. 'Yassine also has to be in Dublin tomorrow, so I persuaded him to come along: we can take the train down together. After all, how often does one get the chance to meet one of the western world's most famous poets?' He clasps Liam's hand in both of his. 'It's a very great honour to meet you.'

Yassine meanwhile has kissed Marie-Claude and is apologising with great courtesy to Liam for his intrusion, but it's plain that McMahon is both amused and curious.

'The honour is all mine,' he says. 'You're more than welcome.'

An extra chair is brought to the table opposite the fireplace. Anton and Marie-Claude help their host to bring through from the kitchen the pot of stew, the plates, the bread; while Patrick uncorks the expensive bottles he's brought with him and keeps up a running commentary on the merits of country cottages, the deficiencies of the airline that brought them here, and the labyrinthine twists of fate that have bound all their lives together.

*

Anton, leaning back in his chair, watches his old friend with amusement – Patrick is on form: he can be relied upon to hold the audience in the palm of his hand. Olivia used to say that he had the face of a Goya matador – she had a habit of likening her friends' features to faces in well-known works of art, something he reminds them of now.

'I was less flatteringly described as a stolid, Flemish burgher – occasionally a minor Gainsborough squire.'

'And Marie-Claude?' Liam asks. 'What were you?'

'One of those secretive Modigliani women,' Patrick answers for her. 'With their long necks and smooth faces!'

Marie-Claude is shaking her head at the silliness of all this, but she smiles at her husband as he hands her the bread. In this light, her face is still youthful, smooth, but underneath the evening make-up her skin is cross-hatched with feathery lines. There are grooves running down either side of her mouth, and a web of fine wrinkles underneath her eyes – those light, greenish-blue eyes that have always given so little away. Anton feels a great wave of tenderness towards her, and wonders, not for the first time, what unknown demons she herself has had to vanquish. He thinks back to their first meeting, that little French girl and the cousin she so clearly hero-worshipped. Once, in the early days of their marriage, he admitted that he'd been briefly smitten with Patrick himself, but she'd just given a small smile and shrugged. 'Oh, everyone's in love with Patrick!' Back then it had all seemed so black and white: you loved women, or you loved men. It was Marie-Claude who said, 'Don't be silly, Anton. You fall in love with a person – it could be a woman, or it could be a man.' Now, all these years later, he wonders if there was rather more than hero-worship involved. Well, it's unlikely that he'll ever know: they've been married thirty-five years and in all that time her calm self-possession has rarely slipped. Occasional impatience, yes – even the odd burst of anger – but on the whole Marie-Claude has dealt with life with grace and stoicism. She will take her secrets to the grave, and for this Anton is deeply grateful. He also very much hopes he won't outlive her.

Patrick appears to be reading his thoughts: 'Well,' he says, 'at least Olivia was spared the hideous slow decline that now faces all the rest of us. My grandfather used to read the obituaries with glee, you know, delighted to have outlived so many of his old cronies. But then, no-one was ever going to shunt him off into some ghastly Home: he had every intention of living to a hundred and being as much of a nuisance as he could.'

'And did he?' Liam enquires.

'Fortunately not. At the age of eighty-nine he tripped over my grandmother's cat in the dark and fell downstairs and broke his neck.' He allows a little pause. 'My grandmother gave orders that the animal should be fed on prawns and cream for the rest of its life.'

Amid the general laughter, more bottles are uncorked, plates refilled, and the talk becomes rambling, relaxed. Liam's hearing is not what it was, more and more these days he misses things, but he thinks Olivia would be gratified to know with what affection she's remembered. The anecdotes come thick and fast: they all have stories, memories, to share. Except for Yassine. Yassine says very little but observes intently. He eats his meal quickly and efficiently, drinks water rather than wine, and then, while the others talk, he sits back with a pad and pencil, and begins to draw.

*

It is long after midnight. Patrick has told his final story and tipped his glass towards Olivia's portrait one last time. 'When all the world was young!' he says. 'And what a long time ago that was!'

Which is the signal for the evening to end. A taxi is called; coats, bags, phones, glasses mislaid then found, and warm if befuddled farewells are made. Then as the lights of the cab disappear down the drive, taking Marie-Claude, Anton, Patrick and Yassine back to their respective hotels and on into the future, Liam walks slowly back towards the empty house. Then changes his mind and turns instead to follow the steps that lead down towards the sea.

On the now deserted pathway, he looks out across the water to the lights that shine on the other side of the lough. Despite what he said to Marie-Claude, there's no sense of any other presence than his own. He knows he's alone, but he talks to her all the same.

'Well,' he says, 'that's the second anniversary over with.' He peers at his watch. 'We're well into tomorrow ... I'm drunk, of course, but it was easier than the first time. Cathartic, really – I haven't spoken as much in years. She's like a well, that Marie-Claude, you can't help dropping the pebbles in.' He sighs, shaking his head. 'You thought she knew about you and Anton, and I'd say you were right, but she's not the sort of woman to let on. Mind you, she could have played with fire as well – your man Yassine would tempt a nun, but in the end it's his work that's always going to matter to him the most. Patrick too: charm incarnate, of course, but ruthless, tough as old boots. They make a good pair, him and Yassine. Anton's different, now – I like him, you know, and Marie-Claude. They were good friends to you. She's been a bit like Teresa, I'd say, bringing up the children, working, keeping it all on an even keel, while the husband gets the glory ... isn't it always the way? I wonder did Teresa ever play with fire? No, I know she didn't. And nor did I, not until the day I met you – well, not really. Fingers slightly burned, once or twice, but nothing serious. Ah well ... Perhaps I'll ask them all back again next year: what do you think? An annual Friends of Olivia dinner? If I'm still here of course ...'

He looks out across the dark rippling water that is running fast with the turning tide, and up at the night sky, where shreds of cloud are flying before the moon. Like elongated ghostly figures, he thinks, racing away to some celestial appointment ... suddenly the starred sky seems to be alive with movement.

'Liv?' he says. 'Is that where you are?'

But at this moment there is the lightest touch of wind against his cheek, and for an instant she is there beside him. He hears her say, 'Enough now, Liam. Go home to bed.'

'Good night then,' he says, but whether to her or to a cat that has just appeared on the wall, he can't be sure. Then he turns away from the sea and climbs back up towards the house.

# Acknowledgements

Thanks to my sister and fellow writer, Catherine Eden, for the exchange of letters that set this novel in motion; to my lovely SCWBI friends for all their encouragement; to the invaluable Averill Buchanan for her assistance and support – and, most of all, to my husband Philip Dufton.

# About the author

Helen Nicholl is the author of *The Traveller's Guide to Love* (Blackstaff Press, 2015) and two children's books, *The Animal Bus* (Shuter and Shooter, 1996) and *Moon's Travelling Circus* (privately published, 2019).

Born and brought up in South Africa, Helen lived and worked in London, Belfast and, for eighteen years, Zimbabwe, before returning to settle permanently in Northern Ireland.

She was also once the model for paintings that hang in private collections around the world.

Printed in Great Britain
by Amazon

38450501R00111